CLUB CSI™:

The Case of the Disappearing Dogs

by David Lewman

Simon Spotlight
New York London Toronto Sydney New Delhi

If you purchased this book without a cover, you should be aware that this book is stolen property. It was reported as "unsold and destroyed" to the publisher, and neither the author nor the publisher has received any payment for this "stripped book."

This book is a work of fiction. Any references to historical events, real people, or real locales are used fictitiously. Other names, characters, places, and incidents are the product of the author's imagination, and any resemblance to actual events or locales or persons, living or dead, is entirely coincidental.

SIMON SPOTLIGHT
An imprint of Simon & Schuster Children's Publishing Division
1230 Avenue of the Americas, New York, New York 10020

Manufactured in the United States of America 0714 OFF
First Edition 10 9 8 7 6 5 4
ISBN 978-1-4424-3396-0 (pbk)
ISBN 978-1-4424-4671-7 (hc)
ISBN 978-1-4424-6689-0 (eBook)
Library of Congress Control Number 2012931484

Chapter 1

Even though Hannah thoroughly enjoyed her mom's delicious rosemary roasted chicken, she was really happy when dinner was finally over, because it meant it was time to go to the park with her dog, Molly.

"C'mon, girl, park time!" Hannah called, and moments later Molly appeared by her side, wiggling with excitement as Hannah attached a leash to her collar.

"I'm meeting up with Corey and Ben after the park to work on homework," she reminded her parents as she headed out the door.

"Bye, honey!" her parents called after her. "Be careful!"

Going to the park after dinner had become a

ritual for Hannah and her dog. But Hannah didn't just play with Molly at the park. Together they were working on agility training. She was teaching her dog to run through an obstacle course and to practice skills like jumping over barriers and weaving between posts.

Molly was becoming very good at agility training. She seemed to love it. And not just for the treats she got as a reward for mastering a skill, though they helped a lot.

"Good girl!" Hannah said after Molly jumped over a low metal bar people used for push-ups and sit-ups. She snapped off a piece of a biscuit and gave it to Molly, who crunched the biscuit and wagged her tail.

"Hannah!"

She turned to see Ben and Corey, her two best friends, approaching. Together the three of them had formed Club CSI, a club dedicated to using the skills they'd learned in forensic science class. Their teacher, Miss Hodges, was their faculty advisor. She was also their favorite teacher at Woodlands Junior High. They felt lucky that she'd moved to their small Nevada town.

"Hi!" Hannah answered, waving. Molly barked a loud greeting.

"Hey, Molly!" Ben said, bending down to greet the bluish-gray dog with a pat on the head. She had a strong body with short fur and a black circle around one eye. She sat right by Hannah, looking as though she were smiling.

"What kind of dog is Molly again?" Corey asked.

Hannah started to answer, but then Corey stopped her. "Wait, don't tell me," he said. "I know you've told me before. I'll remember." He stared at Molly and pursed his lips, thinking. "An Austrian candle dog?"

"She's an Australian cattle dog," Hannah said, shaking her head.

"Oh, right," Corey said, nodding.

"What would a candle dog be, anyway?" Ben asked.

"One that's really bright?" Corey suggested.

Hannah laughed. "Well, she *is* really bright, that's for sure. She knows lots of commands: sit, stay, come, down, over, under . . ."

"I read that dogs can understand two hundred words," Ben said.

"Which ones?" Corey asked.

Ben looked confused. "Which dogs, you mean? All of them."

"No, I mean which words," Corey explained.

"I think it varies from dog to dog," Ben said. "And what language their owner speaks."

"I saw a video of a dog on the Internet saying 'I love you,'" Corey said. "At least, that's what they *claimed* the dog was saying. To me, it sounded more like 'Ah wuh woo.' And I'm not sure the dog really meant it."

Ben turned back to Hannah. "Are you still having problems with Molly ripping things up? And nipping at people's heels?"

"Nope," Hannah said, scratching Molly's back. "No more ripping and nipping. She's been so much better since we started agility training." Molly wagged her tail as Hannah spoke, as if she understood what she was saying. "Australian cattle dogs were bred to herd cattle, so they have a lot of energy. If they don't get enough exercise, they can get destructive. That's what was happening with Molly, but she's much better now."

"I'm kind of the same way," Corey admitted.

"What's agility training, anyway?"

"We'll show you," Hannah said. She found some sticks and then stuck them in the ground, so they looked like a line of poles. "Come on, Molly! Weave!"

With a little encouragement from Hannah, Molly wove in and out of the poles, making her way from one end of the line to the other. When she made it past the last stick, she got another treat from Hannah.

"Good girl!" Hannah cooed, rubbing Molly's ears.

"Very cool," Corey agreed admiringly.

"I've heard that Australian cattle dogs are part dingo," Ben said.

"Yeah, I've heard that too," Hannah said.

"What's a dingo?" Corey asked. "Sounds like some kind of Australian snack item." He did his best Australian accent. "G'day, mate. Have a dingo? They're crunchy and delicious!"

"A dingo is a wild dog found only in Australia," Ben said.

"Or maybe a game," Corey continued, feeling like he was on a roll. "Who's up for a game of dingo? Really fun. You weave in and out of poles. Then you jump over a kangaroo!"

Molly bumped Hannah's leg with her nose. "She wants to do some more training," Hannah reported. "She loves it."

"Is she good at it?" Ben asked.

Hannah led Molly toward a big horizontal cement pipe by the playground. The guys followed. "She's getting good," Hannah said. "In fact, I don't want to brag. . . ."

"Ah, go on," Corey said. "We don't mind a bit."

Hannah pointed toward the pipe. Molly ran straight through it and rushed back to Hannah. For that she got another treat.

"Well," Hannah said, "this past Saturday, Molly competed in a contest sponsored by O'Brien's."

"The pet store?" Ben asked.

Hannah nodded. "Yeah. I think they board dogs too."

"How'd Molly do?" Corey asked.

Hannah couldn't help but grin with pride. "She won! First place!"

"Wow!" Ben said. "Was it an agility contest?"

"No," Hannah said. "Just a general dog contest. But we did a few agility tricks, and the judges were really impressed. Molly was so good! She followed all my commands. And, of course, she was the most

beautiful dog in the contest."

"Of course," Ben said, smiling.

Corey scratched Molly behind her pointed ears. "Way to go, Molly! Did they give you a big cash prize?"

"No cash prize," Hannah said. "But they did give us special organic peanut-butter flavored dog treats. And a sticker to put on our window. It lets the fire department know there's a dog in our house. Everyone got those."

"Mmm, peanut butter," Corey said. "I'll bet Molly was a lot more excited about the treats than she was about the sticker."

Molly bumped Hannah's leg with her nose again, so Hannah gestured for her to go through the pipe again. Molly ran through it, ran back, sat at Hannah's feet, and waited for her treat. She got it.

"Actually," Hannah said, "Molly didn't like the peanut-butter treats. I don't know why. The other dogs seemed to love them."

"Hmm, that's strange," Corey said. "Do you have any of those peanut-butter treats on you? Maybe I should check them out."

"Check them out how?" Ben said. "By eating them?!"

"Maybe," Corey said. "I'm sure they're safe. And maybe they're delicious. As delicious as a dingo!"

"No, these are different treats," Hannah said, holding up one. "These are the kind Molly likes."

The three friends were still laughing about Corey eating dog treats when a cute little dog ran up to Molly. It was a small brown-and-black dog, with a round, furry face and a pink collar. The two dogs sniffed each other and then started to play together.

"Stop! Get that dog away from Princess!"

A teenage girl wearing an oversize red Woodlands High School sweatshirt ran toward them, looking furious. She scooped up the little dog into her arms.

"They're just playing," Hannah said, smiling.

"That dingo would hurt Princess!" the girl insisted. "It's way too wild to play with a little Norwich terrier like my Princess."

Molly sat down with her tongue hanging out, looking friendly.

"First of all, Molly's not an it," Hannah said, trying to stay calm even though the girl was making her mad. "She's a she. And she's not a dingo. She's an Australian cattle dog. She'd never hurt your dog. Look, she likes her!"

The girl ignored Hannah as she stomped away carrying her dog in her arms. "Did that nasty wild animal hurt you, Princess?" she said loud enough for everyone to hear. "Creatures like that shouldn't be allowed in the park. Or the people who own them!"

Hannah watched her go with disbelief. "How rude!" she said. Then she cocked her head to the side, thinking. "Wait a minute," she said. "I recognize that girl. Her name's Lauren. She's in high school."

"And she works at O'Brien's pet supply, doesn't she?" Ben said.

Hannah turned to Ben, surprised. "Yes, but how did you know that? You don't have a pet."

Ben shrugged. "I went in there just the other day. I'm thinking about getting an axolotl."

Corey stared at Ben. "You know, every time you say something like that, I think you're just making up words."

"I didn't make up 'axolotl'!" Ben said. "They're really interesting. They're this kind of salamander from Mexico, and they stay in their larval form all their lives. They have feathery gills that—"

Hannah interrupted before Ben could launch into a long, detailed lecture on Mexican salamanders.

"Even though Lauren works at O'Brien's, she entered her dog in the contest last weekend."

Corey made a face. "That doesn't seem fair. I mean, she'd know the judges, wouldn't she? Her dog would be a shoo-in. Although dogs usually don't wear shoes. So, I guess, a paw-in?"

Molly tilted her head toward Corey, as if she were listening to what he had to say.

"Well, she didn't win," Hannah said, looking satisfied. "Her dog came in second to Molly, and Lauren wasn't happy about that. That's probably why she was so mean, pretending to think Molly's a wild dingo. She knows better than that. She had to have heard them call Molly an Australian cattle dog at the contest."

"Man, it's a dog-eat-dog world," Corey observed. Then he looked at Molly and added, "No offense."

Molly gave Corey a friendly look, as if to say, *None taken.*

Chapter 2

Ben, Hannah, and Corey walked Molly back to Hannah's house on their way to Ben's. Before she left Molly inside the front hallway, Hannah knelt down and took Molly's face in her hands. "You be a good girl, and I'll see you real soon," she whispered. Molly licked Hannah's face.

As they walked down the sidewalk, Hannah could hear Molly barking inside the house. She only barked a couple of times, but the barking still got to Hannah. She hated leaving Molly. But she knew Ben's mom was allergic to dogs, so she couldn't bring Molly over to his house while they worked on their forensics homework.

"Did you happen to bring any of those peanut-butter treats with you?" Corey asked as they headed

toward Ben's house. "I'm starving."

"You *do* know those are *dog* treats, right?" Hannah asked, amazed at Corey's never-ending appetite.

"Fine," Corey said. "If there's nothing to eat, then you guys will have to distract me from my hunger."

"With what?" Ben asked. "Interesting facts about the axolotl?"

"I was thinking more along the lines of . . . *a race*!" Corey shouted as he took off running.

Hannah and Ben continued walking at a leisurely pace.

Corey jogged back to them. "What's the matter? Don't you want to race?"

"No," Hannah said.

"Why not?" Corey asked.

"Because we already know you'll win," Ben said. "You're the fastest."

Corey smiled. "Thank you. But who knows? Maybe I'm having a bad day. Or maybe one of you will have a really excellent day!"

Ben and Hannah just kept on walking. Corey slowed to a walk.

"I'm starving," he said. "Oh, great. I'm not distracted at all."

"One of the many interesting characteristics of the axolotl is its—" Ben started to say. Corey sprinted ahead.

"See you at Ben's house!" he called back to them.

Ben led the way up the stairs to his room. It had a bed in it, so technically it was a bedroom. But it looked more like a laboratory. There were test tubes, flasks, chemistry sets, microscopes . . .

"Why do you have *two* microscopes?" Corey asked. "One for each eye?"

"I don't have two microscopes," Ben said.

"Yes, you do!" Corey insisted, pointing. "Right there, and over there! One, two!"

"I have *three* microscopes," Ben said calmly. "There's one in the closet. When I was seven, my parents and my aunt forgot to talk about what they were going to get me for Christmas."

"Okay," Hannah said. "That explains two microscopes, not three."

"Then a few years later," Ben continued, "my parents decided to get me a better microscope—more powerful. So now I have three."

Corey pulled a beat-up-looking notebook out of

his backpack and brushed cookie crumbs off it. "Well, we might need three microscopes to get through all this forensics homework. Miss Hodges kind of piled it on this time."

Hannah pulled a much neater-looking notebook out of her backpack. "This is for the unit on analyzing materials, right?"

"Right," Ben agreed, reaching for his copy of the forensics textbook.

"It's unbelievable how many different materials you can find at a crime scene and then analyze in the lab," Corey said, looking through his notes from class. "Glass, soil, rope, wood, tape . . ."

"Polymers," Ben added.

Corey stared at him. "You know, if you're going to make up words, you should at least make them *sound* real."

Ben laughed. "Again, I didn't make up that word. A polymer is a compound. It has large molecules, made up of smaller molecules."

Corey shook his head. "You see, Ben, the whole point of using words is to make people understand you. Not to confuse them."

Hannah waved for their attention. "Why don't

we start with glass? We're supposed to know why an investigator might collect broken glass from a crime scene."

Corey raised his hand. "I know. Safety. You don't want to cut your feet."

Ben squinted at Corey in disbelief. "So you're investigating the crime scene in your bare feet?"

"You might," Corey said. "Like, if the crime happened at a beach. Or a pool. Or in some temple or something where they make you take off your shoes."

"But you'd leave your footprints everywhere!" Ben protested.

"Not if I tiptoed!"

"Toe prints, then!"

"Well, maybe I could hover over the crime scene in a harness!"

"Then you wouldn't have to worry about cutting your feet on the glass!"

Sometimes Ben had the feeling Corey was trying to drive him crazy.

Hannah tried to get them back on track. "What I meant was, why would you collect broken glass as evidence?"

Ben said, "The broken glass at the crime scene might match glass on a suspect. Bits of glass could be stuck on a suspect's clothing or in their hair."

Corey frowned, thinking. "Makes sense. A criminal might break a glass window or door to get in somewhere. Or it might be dark, so he'd bump into a vase or something and break it."

"The trick," Ben continued, "is to match the glass at the crime scene with glass on the subject."

"Right," Hannah said. "So what kind of analysis can you do on glass to try to make a match?"

Corey flipped through his notes again. "Oh! I got this. Um, you can check the color of the glass. Whether or not it reflects light. And its shape, like whether or not it's curved."

"You can also analyze the glass's density," Ben said, nodding in agreement. "And its chemical makeup."

"Correct," Hannah confirmed. "Miss Hodges also talked about how you can try to put two pieces of broken glass together to see if they fit, like pieces of a puzzle."

Corey looked confused. "You know what part I don't get? All that stuff about the cracks in a piece

of glass. I sort of get that you can look at a piece of glass and figure out which way a bullet went through it, but I don't really see how."

"What have you got in your notes?" Hannah asked, craning her neck to see what Corey had written in his notebook.

"Umm . . . some doodles of a bullet going through a window," Corey said. "And then I drew this cool little bullet with arms, legs, and a face. And a cowboy hat."

Hannah and Ben laughed and then consulted their notes and tried to explain the way lines in a piece of broken glass can tell an investigator a lot about how the glass broke. Ben even found a cracked picture frame and put it under the microscope, so they could look at the fracture lines. By the time they were finished, Corey understood the lesson perfectly.

"So much for glass," Corey declared, looking up from the microscope and stretching. "What's next?"

"Soil?" Hannah suggested.

"Ah," Corey said, grinning. "Now there's a subject I know something about."

"Such as?" Ben asked.

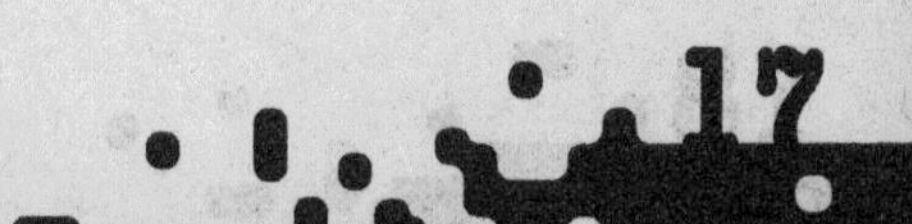

Corey stroked his chin, trying to look like a wise professor. "Soil," he began seriously, "is another word for 'dirt.' Dirt is what makes things dirty. It's mostly found on the ground or under grass or in the corners of my bedroom."

"Excellent," Ben said. "You're clearly an expert."

"Thank you," Corey replied, with a slight bow of his head.

"If you're trying to match two soil samples, what might you compare?" Hannah asked.

"Color," Corey said. "With pretty much any material, you can always look at the color. When I take a forensics quiz, 'color' is almost always the first word I write in every answer." He turned to Ben. "That's a little test-taking tip for you. No charge."

"Thanks," Ben said dryly.

"You're right about checking the color of the soil, Corey," Hannah said. "What else?"

"Texture," Ben suggested. "Composition. You can measure the pH."

"What's that?" Corey asked.

"The acidity of the soil," Ben explained.

"Oh, right," Corey said. "Like pH-balanced shampoo. Which makes a lot of sense. You wouldn't want to wash your hair with acid. Unless you had really ugly hair."

"You could do a chemical analysis of the soil," Ben added. "And you could examine the soil under a microscope."

"Shall we?" Corey said, gesturing toward one of Ben's microscopes.

"Okay," Ben said. "But where will we get the soil? Should I go out in the yard and get some?"

"No need," Hannah said, smiling. "We've got Corey's backpack."

"Very funny," Corey said. Then he looked at his filthy backpack. "Actually, you're right. Guess I shouldn't have thrown it in the mud at the park!"

When they put some dirt on a slide and examined it under the microscope, they could see some of the tiny crystals and minerals that made up the soil. It was amazing how complicated something as common as dirt could be when a person looked at it really closely.

The three friends reviewed what Miss Hodges had told them about rope, wood, tape, and other materials. In what seemed like no time at all, Ben's mom called up that it was getting late—time for

Hannah and Corey to head home.

"And for Ben to take out the trash!" she added, and Ben groaned. And then Hannah and Corey groaned, too, because the same chore awaited them at home.

When Hannah walked in the front doorway of her house, Molly ran up to her, barking with joy.

"Molly!" Hannah's dad said sharply, coming pretty close to barking himself. "Please be quiet!"

Hannah was able to stop Molly's barking by petting her, stroking her soft fur all the way from her head to her tail.

"So how was the study session?" Mrs. Miller asked.

"Good, Mom!" Hannah replied. "We went over a lot of material. About materials."

"What kind of materials?" her mom asked. "You mean, like fabrics?"

"Stuff you might find at a crime scene," Hannah explained. "Wood, glass, soil . . ."

"I don't quite see the appeal of a crime scene," Mrs. Miller said, frowning. "Has Club CSI got another case already?"

Hannah shook her head. "No, there haven't been any crimes at school lately. Unfortunately."

Hannah's mom looked a little shocked. "I'm pretty sure it's a *good* thing that your school's been free of crimes. I'm relieved that your club hasn't taken on another case."

"Why?" Hannah asked, reaching for the brush to use on Molly's coat.

"It makes me nervous having you investigate crimes," Mrs. Miller said. "It seems dangerous."

Hannah brushed Molly's back. When she reached a certain spot, Molly happily tapped the floor with her back paw. "We're really careful," Hannah assured her mother. "We wouldn't do anything dangerous."

"I just don't know why you now seem so much more interested in forensics than in ballet," her mom continued. "What do you think, Dave?" she asked, nodding toward Hannah's father.

"I think it's good for Hannah to have a lot of interests. And you're not giving up on ballet, right, honey?" Mr. Miller replied, smiling at his daughter.

"No, I'm just exploring other interests," Hannah said. And then eager to change the subject she added, "I'm going to take Molly for her last trip outside before bed."

"Don't walk too far," Mrs. Miller advised. "It's dark out."

"I won't," Hannah said, putting on her jacket.

"Don't worry," Hannah heard her dad tell her mom. "She's got Molly with her. She'll be fine."

Hannah got Molly's leash from the closet. The minute Molly saw it, she started wriggling with excitement about going outside again.

The two of them headed out the front door. Molly wanted to go first, but Hannah made her wait until she went through the door. She'd seen a guy on TV talk about how important this was for establishing yourself as the pack leader.

Outside, it was dark but not cold. Hannah and Molly headed down the sidewalk. Molly trotted along at Hannah's side, always on her left.

They passed a neighbor walking his dog. The neighbor smiled and nodded at Hannah. The two dogs looked at each other, but kept right on walking with their owners.

"Molly, you want to run?" Hannah asked. The minute Hannah said Molly's name, she looked up at Hannah. When she heard the word "run," she started to move faster.

Hannah laughed. "'Run' must be one of the two hundred words you understand," she said as they started to sprint.

Molly ran fast. It was hard to keep up with her. No matter how much exercise Hannah gave her dog during the day, she still had lots of energy at night. She was out in front of Hannah, pulling the leash tight.

They raced for a couple of blocks, but then Hannah was out of breath from trying to keep up with Molly. "Okay, Molly," she said, "let's slow down." They slowed from a run to a walk. Molly seemed a little disappointed, but at least this gave her more of a chance to sniff the sidewalk. And the fire hydrants. And the trees.

After another block of walking, they turned around and headed back home. In the middle of the walk, Hannah let Molly run for one more block.

As soon as they were back inside the house, Molly sat down, waiting for Hannah to unclip the leash

from her collar. "Good girl," Hannah said. She'd trained Molly to sit down as soon as she got back inside the house, and she was pleased whenever Molly remembered her training.

Just as Hannah was heading upstairs to get ready for bed, her mom asked, "Hannah, did you remember to set out the garbage?" The garbage! She'd almost forgotten it was the night before trash day.

"Sorry," she replied. "I'll go back out and do it right now."

"Thank you!" Mrs. Miller said. "I appreciate it."

Hannah walked through the kitchen and out the back door. As she crossed the yard to the gate, she thought about what her mother had brought up before.

Hannah still loved ballet, but she had decided recently that she didn't want to be a ballerina when she grew up. It seemed awfully hard to get into a ballet company, and then you could only dance for a few years until you were too old. Most ballerinas went on to teach dance when they got older, but that wasn't what Hannah wanted to do when she grew up.

She was much more interested in the idea of

investigating crime scenes. She loved how all the different information came together. A clue here and a clue there, and you could figure out how the crime was committed. And maybe even who did it.

Hannah opened the gate, got the trash can, and pulled it past the opened gate door. She rolled it through the yard, being careful not to bump against any of the safety lights lining the walkway. She'd forgotten to turn the lights on before she came outside, and they were a little hard to see in the dark.

Still thinking about her future, she wheeled the trash can to the front curb.

She set the garbage in place for the truck to pick up early the next morning. Then she went back inside the house, turned on the yard's security lights and the walkway's safety lights, and went to bed.

Chapter 4

"Why am I dressed like a ballerina?" Hannah asked herself. The policemen and detectives all stared at her as she walked up to the crime scene.

She wanted to start taking photos of the area inside the yellow caution tape, but realized she didn't have her camera. Her ballerina costume didn't have any pockets.

A detective in a brown raincoat came up to her. "Are you here to investigate a crime scene or to dance *Swan Lake*?" he asked. The policemen all laughed. Hannah blushed. Then music started to play . . .

Hannah woke from the dream to the sound of

her alarm clock's radio, tuned to her favorite radio station. *That was weird,* she thought. *But then, pretty much* all *dreams are weird.*

Another thing was weird too. As she got up, she realized a sound was missing.

Every morning, when she woke up, the first thing she heard was Molly outside her bedroom door. Her dog was eager to see her, so she'd bump the door with her nose. Nudge it with her head. Even whine a little. Anything to get Hannah to come out of her bedroom.

But this morning, there was no noise at the door. No bumping. No nudging. No whining. Nothing.

Where was Molly?

Still a little sleepy, Hannah walked across her bedroom to the door and then opened it.

No Molly.

"Molly?" Hannah asked. "Where are you?" She looked up and down the upstairs hallway, but didn't see any sign of her dog.

"Molly, come!" Hannah called. "Come!" That usually brought Molly running. Hannah whistled loudly. That *always* brought Molly running. But not this time.

"Hannah?" her mom called from downstairs. "Are you up?"

"Yeah, Mom, I'm up," Hannah answered. "Have you seen Molly?"

"Come on downstairs," her mom called.

Hannah hurried down the stairs and into the kitchen. Her parents were both sitting at the table. Molly wasn't there.

From her parents' faces, Hannah could tell something was wrong. "What's the matter?" she asked. "Where's Molly?"

"She's missing," her dad said gently. "She's not in the house, and she's not in the yard."

Hannah felt her stomach lurch. Missing? She thought she was going to cry. "How?" she managed to say. "How can she be missing?"

Mrs. Miller put her arm around Hannah's shoulders. "The gate was open," her dad explained. "She must have gone out into the yard through her doggy door and then just wandered out the open gate."

"Wandered?" Hannah said. "That doesn't sound like Molly. Molly doesn't wander."

Then Mr. Miller asked if Hannah might have accidentally left the gate open when she moved the trash can the night before. She shook her head. "I'm positive I closed the gate. Positive."

Hannah's parents could see she was upset, so they didn't push her about leaving the gate open. But Hannah could tell they didn't believe her. She felt tears of frustration stinging her eyes.

She was going to prove she didn't.

But even more important, she was going to get her dog back. "I think Club CSI just got a case," she said, sounding determined.

Before her parents could say anything more, Hannah ran upstairs to text Ben and Corey, telling them that Molly was missing. And that she was pretty sure someone must have opened the gate and dog-napped her dog.

A moment later Hannah's phone rang, and it was Ben. He told her how sorry he was that Molly was missing, but said that Club CSI would find her for sure. "We'll start our investigation right after school," he promised.

"I wish I didn't have to go to school today," Hannah said sadly. "I wish I could just spend the whole day searching for Molly. I hope whoever took her is taking good care of her. I'm so worried."

"It'll be okay," Ben reassured her. "But I think you should secure the crime scene to make sure it isn't disturbed."

Hannah thought that was a good idea. She thanked Ben, told him she'd see him at school, and hung up.

She wanted to secure the crime scene right away. She didn't want anyone messing up any clues that might lead to Molly's recovery. But she didn't have any yellow crime-scene tape. There wasn't time to go to a store. She wasn't sure which store sold crime-scene tape, anyway.

What could she use? She looked around her room.

A few minutes later Hannah's mom was surprised to look out the kitchen window to see her daughter tying pink ribbon around the gate.

"Why is Hannah tying ballet slipper ribbons around the gate?" she asked her husband. "Is it some kind of tribute to Molly, like tying a yellow ribbon around a tree until someone comes home?"

Mr. Miller looked out the window. "No," he said. "I'm pretty sure our daughter is using pink ribbons from her ballet slippers to secure the crime scene."

"Crime?" Mrs. Miller repeated. "What crime?

Hannah left the gate open, and Molly ran away. That's a mistake, or an accident, but it's not a crime."

Mr. Miller shook his head. "I don't think that's how Hannah sees it," he said.

Outside, Hannah finished tying the pink ribbons around the gate. *There,* she thought to herself. *That'll have to do until we can investigate thoroughly after school.*

As she headed inside to get ready for school, she thought for the millionth time, *Where is Molly?*

Chapter 5

At school Hannah met Corey and Ben near the end of a hallway that didn't get used much anymore. It was a good place to talk. They usually sat on the floor by the old wooden display cases full of sports trophies. But today they were standing. Hannah was too upset to sit. She paced.

"It's just not like Molly to run away," Hannah said. "She loves to be with us. If she could, she'd follow me around all day. She'd even come with me to school."

"She's probably smarter than some of the kids in my homeroom," Corey joked. He could tell Hannah was feeling really bad about her missing dog, and he wanted to say something funny to try to cheer her up.

"Since she's an Australian cattle dog, I'll bet she likes to keep you and your family all together, like a little herd of sheep," Ben suggested. He thought maybe he could make Hannah feel better by distracting her with interesting facts. It always worked for him.

"I definitely didn't leave the gate open," Hannah said firmly. "Someone opened it and took Molly. I'm sure she didn't run away!"

Ben wasn't positive about this theory, since they didn't have all the facts yet. But he didn't want to disagree with Hannah out loud. It'd probably just upset her more. "We'll find her," he said.

"I can sympathize," Corey said. "Once I had a pet frog run away. Well, hop away."

"Molly didn't run away," Hannah repeated. "Someone took her."

"Come on," Ben said, realizing there was nothing he or Corey could say to make Hannah feel better. "If we don't hurry, we'll be late to forensics."

"Today we're going to continue working on analysis of materials found at a crime scene," Miss Hodges

said, standing at the front of the classroom. "I'm sure you all reviewed the chapter in your textbook last night."

Some students nodded. Others sat quietly, hoping to avoid being called on.

"Let's start with a very common material we see all around us: wood," she went on. "If you were trying to match wood from a crime scene with wood found on a suspect, or in their house, what might you compare first?"

"The color," Corey said, giving Ben a quick smile.

"Yes, you could start with the color," Miss Hodges agreed. She wrote "color" on the dry-erase board. "Color is one of the first things we see when we're doing a macroanalysis. Remember, 'macro' means 'large'—the kind of things we can see with our eyes, without having to use a magnifying glass or a microscope."

Miss Hodges passed out several sample pieces of different kinds of wood for the students to examine. They passed them around, taking notes on their color and texture.

"Can anyone can tell me what dendrochronology is?" Miss Hodges asked. She looked around the room, smiling. "Have I stumped you all?"

Ben raised his hand, and Miss Hodges called on him. "Dating something by counting the rings in a tree," he said.

"What would you know about dating?" Ricky Collins asked, getting a laugh out of his buddies. Ricky was a big kid who acted tough, but he actually wasn't so bad once you got to know him.

"Exactly right, Ben," Miss Hodges said, shooting a look at Ricky. "'Dendro' means 'tree,' and chronology has to do with dates. Many trees add a layer every year. When you cut through the tree, you can see the rings, indicating how many years the tree has been growing. You can often see this in a tree stump."

Miss Hodges showed the class how you could still see the rings of a tree in a piece of cut wood, like a board.

"If the number of rings match in two different pieces of wood, that could be a valuable piece of evidence," she explained.

Next she had the students examine small samples of wood under the microscopes. By looking at the cells, experts could identify what type of wood they were looking at.

"Has anyone ever heard of Charles Lindbergh?" Miss Hodges asked.

Ben glanced at Hannah. He knew Hannah had done a report on the famous aviator in sixth grade. But Hannah didn't raise her hand. She was staring out the window, probably still thinking about Molly.

Another student, Rachel, told about how Charles Lindbergh flew across the Atlantic Ocean all by himself.

"Good, Rachel," Miss Hodges said. "Now, has anyone heard what happened to the Lindbergh baby?"

Ben couldn't help but look at Hannah again. He was certain she knew the answer. But she still wasn't participating in the class discussion.

"Wasn't he kidnapped?" Ricky said. Crimes interested him. He'd watched a show on TV about the Lindbergh baby being kidnapped.

"Yes!" Miss Hodges said with a smile, happy that Ricky had finally contributed something to the discussion besides a joke or a sarcastic comment. "And the man who helped convict the kidnapper was an expert on wood. By examining the wooden ladder left at the crime scene by the kidnapper, he was able to figure out what kind of wood the ladder was made of.

"That helped the police figure out where the wood for the ladder had been bought," she continued. "The expert also told the police to look for a piece of wood that had been cut out and used for part of the ladder. When they looked in the suspect's attic, they found where he'd cut out the piece of wood."

Miss Hodges picked up one of the small wood samples, tossed it up, and caught it. "So forensic examination of wood can lead directly to the conviction of a criminal. Of course nowadays, we have much more sophisticated tools for analyzing wood."

She went on to explain something called Laser-Induced Breakdown Spectroscopy, or LIBS. Corey struggled a bit to follow this lesson, but from what he could tell, it seemed to involve shooting a laser at a piece of wood to get a puff of vapor. Then you analyzed the colors in the light from the vapor to figure out what chemicals were in the wood. Or something like that. Corey made a note to ask Ben later to help him with that part of the lesson.

"LIBS can give us something like a fingerprint for the wood," Miss Hodges explained. "We can match pieces of wood with pretty good certainty that they came from the same place."

"When would you use this?" Ricky asked. "When someone killed someone with a log?"

"You might," Miss Hodges said, nodding. "But in one case, a murderer tried to burn the body of his victim. The forensic examiners were able to match the charred logs to some logs the murderer had brought to a party. Based partly on this evidence, the murderer was convicted."

"I guess his *bark* was worse than his bite," Ricky joked. Several students laughed. Hannah didn't. To her, right now, there was nothing funny about barking.

"All right," Miss Hodges said. "I think that's enough about wood for now. Let's talk about rope."

As Miss Hodges explained about different kinds of rope and how they were made, Hannah continued to stare out the window. She heard very little of what the teacher said about the materials used in ropes and how they were woven together.

And she heard almost nothing Miss Hodges

said about knots and how people tend to tie the same type of knot in the same way over and over. When the teacher broke the class into groups and had them tie knots to see how each student did it, Hannah barely participated. Usually she was the leader of whatever group she was in.

Ben and Corey both noticed Hannah was not paying attention. It wasn't like her at all. They exchanged a worried look.

"We've got to find Molly," Corey whispered to Ben during the group exercise on tying knots.

Ben nodded. "We'll start looking right after school," he said.

Chapter 6

The minute the final bell rang, Hannah ran to her locker. At lunch she'd told Corey and Ben to meet her there at the end of the school day.

She got out everything she needed, slammed her locker door closed, and spun the dial on the lock. Then she turned around and looked down the hall, impatiently waiting for her two friends.

They soon came jogging up, ready to go. "Okay," Hannah said. "Let's get to my house and investigate the crime scene." She turned and started to walk rapidly down the hall.

Ben and Corey hurried after her. "Wait, Hannah," Ben said. "I was thinking that first we should go by the animal shelter and see if anyone's turned Molly in."

Hannah wheeled around. "Why would someone steal Molly and then turn her in to the animal shelter?"

Ben hesitated. He knew Hannah was upset about her missing dog, so he didn't like to disagree with her. But he was also a big believer in facts.

"Well," he said gently, "at this point we don't actually *know* that someone stole Molly. If she did happen to get loose, someone might have picked her up and taken her to the shelter." He made a point of saying "get loose" instead of "run away," since he knew Hannah didn't think Molly would ever run away.

"It might be worth a shot," Corey said, agreeing with Ben. "Maybe she's at the pound, wondering where you are and why you haven't come to pick her up yet!"

That worked. To Hannah, the idea of her dog sitting alone in a cage, waiting to be rescued, was unbearable. "Let's go," she said.

Lindsay, the pretty young woman at the front counter, shook her head. "No Australian cattle dogs here," she said. "That's a distinctive breed. I'd remember if one came in."

"Might someone have brought the dog in before

you came on duty?" Ben asked.

Lindsay smiled. She knew how much people worried about their dogs. She liked to make them feel better whenever she could. Her favorite moments were when owners were reunited with their lost dogs.

"If you'd like, you can come in the back and check for yourself," she offered kindly. "If your dog is here, we certainly want you to find her."

"Thank you," Hannah said. "I'm really worried about her."

Lindsay led them through a doorway to a long room lined with cages. As they walked in, dogs started barking.

They walked down the room, looking in the cages on both sides and checking to make sure they saw every dog. There were dogs in every shape and size, every color and pattern.

But no Molly.

She was such an unusual dog, with her bluish fur and the black circle around her eye, there was no mistaking any of the dogs in the shelter for Molly.

Hannah turned around, letting out a big sigh. "You were right. She's not here."

"I'm sorry," Lindsay replied. "You're welcome to fill out one of our forms with a description of your dog and all your contact information. If someone brings in Molly, we'll call you right away."

Hannah nodded. She didn't have much faith that anyone would bring Molly to the animal shelter, but she was grateful to the woman for being so nice. And she appreciated her remembering Molly's name.

At Hannah's house the members of Club CSI passed through the kitchen on their way to the backyard. Her mom was sitting at the table, a cup of coffee in front of her. "I was thinking that maybe we should go to the animal shelter to make sure someone hasn't turned in Molly," she said.

"We just came from the shelter," Hannah said. "She isn't there."

"Oh," Mrs. Miller replied, clearly disappointed. "Well, in that case, I want to show you something."

She got up and walked over to the counter. She held up a piece of paper for them to see. It was a missing dog poster she had created on the computer. The poster said there was a five-hundred-dollar

reward for anyone who brought Molly home.

"Thanks, Mom," Hannah said. "That's incredibly generous of you and Dad."

"Wow, five hundred bucks!" Corey exclaimed. "I hope I'm the one who finds her!"

"Well, honey," Mrs. Miller said, "we know how much Molly means to you. To all of us." She picked up a stack of paper. "I printed out a bunch of posters for you three to put up around the neighborhood."

"That's great," Hannah said. "But first we're going to investigate the crime scene."

Mrs. Miller sighed. She didn't believe that the yard really qualified as a "crime scene." But she knew a thorough investigation was important to her daughter, and she certainly didn't want to upset her further. "All right," she said. "Go ahead. And don't worry—it's secure," she said with an encouraging smile. "No one has dared to cross the ballet ribbons. I kept an eye on the yard all day for you."

"Ballet ribbons?" Corey asked, puzzled.

Outside, Ben and Corey spotted the pink ribbons Hannah had used that morning to secure the scene.

"Nicely done," Ben said, admiring Hannah's ingenuity.

"Well, I didn't have any yellow crime-scene tape," Hannah said.

"I like this better," Corey remarked, poking the pink ribbon. "Festive."

Before they started investigating the gate and the yard, they made a quick plan, the way Miss Hodges had taught them. First they divided the crime scene into three sections, assigning one-third of the area to each investigator.

Next they put on plastic gloves and made sure each of them had plastic bags and jars ready, to store any evidence they found, as well as tweezers to collect the evidence. Then they took pictures to record exactly how the scene looked.

After a few minutes Ben asked, "Pictures done?" Hannah and Corey nodded. "All right. Let's find some evidence."

The three of them began to scan the area carefully, bending over to inspect the ground. They were careful to examine each bit of earth before they stepped on it.

They stared at the ground, working in silence.

Corey was the first to speak. "I think I've got something!" he said, excited.

"What is it?" Hannah asked, standing up straight. She wanted to rush over to see what Corey'd found, but knew she shouldn't walk all over that part of the yard before he finished examining it.

Corey squatted down and peered at the grass. "Crumbs. Brownish-orange crumbs."

"Crumbs might have been there before Molly disappeared," Ben pointed out, frowning.

"True," Corey replied. "But one of these is shaped kind of like a piece of a dog biscuit. You want to come over and look at these, Hannah?"

Hannah started over. "Watch your step," Ben reminder her.

Hannah reached the spot next to Corey and squatted down to examine the crumbs. "Yeah," she said, nodding. "These definitely look like they came from a dog biscuit. Like someone dropped a treat and then accidentally stepped on it."

"Could it just be one of Molly's old treats?" Ben asked.

Hannah looked closer, then shook her head. "I don't think so. They're the wrong color. " Then she realized something. "You know what these crumbs look like?"

"Cookie crumbs?" Corey asked.

Hannah shot him a look.

"Sorry," he apologized. "I'm starving. We came straight from school. We totally skipped our after-school snack."

"Since when do we have an after-school snack?" Hannah asked.

Corey looked as though he couldn't believe what she was saying. "We always have an after-school snack!" he insisted. "Well, to be fair, you guys aren't always there."

"You were saying what the crumbs looked like," Ben prompted Hannah.

"Right," Hannah said. "The color and the texture of the bigger pieces remind me of the peanut-butter treats they handed out at the dog contest last weekend. . . . The ones I told you about, the ones Molly didn't like! "

They decided the crumbs were worth collecting as possible evidence. Corey held open a plastic bag while Hannah carefully picked up the crumbs with tweezers and put them into the bag.

They resumed scanning the ground for evidence. Ben was the next to speak up. "I think I may

have found something here."

He'd spotted small pieces of glass on the walkway. Nearby, one of the low safety lights was knocked over.

"The glass is thin and curved," Ben said. "It looks like it came from a broken lightbulb, probably from this safety light. Was the light broken before?"

"No," Hannah said. "Definitely not."

"Sounds like evidence to me," Corey observed.

Ben pulled a plastic jar from his backpack.

"Careful," Hannah warned. "Don't cut yourself."

"I won't," Ben said. He carefully gathered the glass fragments with his tweezers and put them into the jar. Then he sealed the jar, labeled it with a marker, and placed it back in his backpack.

Two pieces of evidence. Hannah was feeling encouraged. She was also eager to find something herself. Just as she was scanning the last section of her assigned area, she spotted something.

A footprint.

Or, rather, since it didn't look like a print from a bare foot, a shoe print.

"I've got a shoe print over here!" she called out, excited.

"Man's shoe or woman's shoe?" Corey asked.

"Man's," she said. "I think."

"Could it be your dad's?" Ben asked.

Hannah bent down and examined the shoe print more closely. "I don't think so," she said. "It looks really big." She snapped a photo of the shoe print with her phone's camera.

Corey and Ben joined Hannah for a closer look. "How do we collect a shoe print?" Corey asked. "Miss Hodges hasn't covered this yet in class. Fingerprints, yes. Shoe prints, no."

Ben smiled. "I've got this." He turned to Hannah. "Do you think your mom will let us have some flour and water?"

"Sure," Hannah said.

"Great idea!" Corey added. "We'll make an after-school snack, and then our brains will perk up, and we'll think of what to do about this shoe print! But, dude, I gotta say—that's the worst cookie recipe I've ever heard. You forgot the sugar and the butter and the chocolate chips. . . ."

"It's not a snack recipe," Ben explained patiently. "It's a simple recipe for plaster of Paris. We're going to make a cast of the shoe print."

Corey looked confused. "How do you know about making casts of shoe prints? We haven't covered that in forensics yet."

Hannah laughed for the first time that day. "How do you think? He read ahead in the textbook. Right?"

Ben looked embarrassed. "Yeah," he admitted. "It just looked really interesting. Also, when I was a kid, I went to Dinosaur Camp, and we made casts of dinosaur footprints."

"Wow," Corey joked. "A camp for dinosaurs. The food bill must have been tremendous."

The members of Club CSI hurried into the kitchen to borrow flour, warm water, a bowl, plastic wrap, and a spoon from Hannah's mom. They mixed the plaster and carefully poured it into the shoe print. Then they covered it with the plastic wrap.

"It'll have to dry overnight," Ben said. "There's no rain predicted, so it should be okay."

They'd collected three excellent pieces of evidence: the crumbs, the lightbulb fragments, and the shoe print. But what did they add up to?

Hannah hurried back into the kitchen, excited by Club CSI's findings. "Mom! We found a broken light, dog-treat crumbs, and a shoe print!"

"I figured you found a shoe print," Mrs. Miller said. "That's what you needed the flour and water for, right?"

"Right," Ben confirmed, impressed that Hannah's mom knew about plaster shoe-print molds. "Thanks again for those. The plaster cast should be dry by morning."

"You're welcome," Mrs. Miller said. "But what's this about a broken light?"

"One of the safety lights lining the walkway was broken," Corey explained.

"We have to analyze all the evidence, but my working theory is that someone opened the gate last night. They came in the yard and tried to tempt Molly out through her pet door with a treat. And they broke the light, either on their way in or on their way out," Hannah summed up.

"Okay," Hannah's mom said slowly. "But isn't it possible that you broke the light yourself when you rolled the garbage can through the yard? And you just didn't notice?"

Hannah shook her head. "I'm sure I'd notice if I broke a light. I'd have heard it break."

"Were the lights on when you rolled the trash through?" Mrs. Miller asked.

Hannah thought a minute. "No," she said. "I turned them on after I came back inside, before I went to bed."

"So it was dark in the yard, and maybe you didn't notice the broken light," Mrs. Miller suggested gently.

"But what about the broken dog biscuit?" Hannah pointed out. "And the shoe print?"

"May I see the biscuit?" Hannah's mom asked. Corey dug the evidence bag out of his pocket and handed it to her. She held up the plastic bag and looked at its contents.

"I guess these could be crumbs from a dog biscuit," she relented. "But they also could be from just about anything. And who knows how long they've been out in the yard?"

Ben could see Hannah was getting frustrated, so he spoke up. "We'll have to analyze them in the lab to try to figure out what they are," he said.

Mrs. Miller handed the bag back to Corey. "Might the shoe print be one of your father's?" she asked.

"It didn't look like it," Hannah said. "We could compare the shoe print to one of Dad's shoes."

"We'll have to wait until the plaster cast dries," Ben reminded them. "Right now the shoe print is covered by the flour mixture."

Hannah's mom picked up the stack of missing dog posters. "Honey, I know you want to do your investigation. And I'm trying to support you with that. But I'd still like for you and your friends to put up these posters. Your dad and I think that's our best chance of bringing Molly home."

"But, Mom," Hannah protested. "What if whoever lured Molly out of the house sees the poster? Instead of being punished for dognapping, they'll get rewarded!"

"Hannah, enough," her mom said firmly. "We all want Molly to come home. Please go outside and put up these posters."

Hannah, Ben, and Corey walked down the front sidewalk from Hannah's house carrying the posters. They also had a stapler, tape, nails, and a hammer.

"I still think this is a bad idea," Hannah grumbled. "Claiming a reward may be exactly what the dognapper had in mind from the very beginning."

"Maybe we should hang the posters in places no one will see," Corey suggested. "Like on the bottoms of garbage cans."

"I think Hannah's parents would notice right away," Ben said.

"Do they always go around looking at the bottoms of garbage cans?" Corey asked.

"I mean, I think they'd notice if they drove around their neighborhood and didn't see a single poster," Ben explained.

Ben secretly agreed with Hannah's mom. He knew that offering a reward was a good way to motivate people to look for a missing pet. He didn't want to tell Hannah he agreed with her mom, though, because he knew it would probably just upset her more.

Working together, they soon had put up a bunch of the posters on telephone poles. A few store owners let them put up the posters in their windows.

As they made their way around the neighborhood, they noticed that several of the houses had stickers in their windows announcing A DOG LIVES HERE. They were the same stickers given away at the dog contest, letting the fire department know which houses had dogs living in them.

They were heading down the sidewalk, looking for a good place to hang another poster, when they saw Lauren coming toward them wearing her big red sweatshirt. She was walking Princess on a pink leash.

"Hi, Lauren," Corey said. He was never too shy to say hi to anyone whose name he knew. Ben envied him a little for that.

"Hello?" Lauren said. It was a question, not a greeting. It meant, "Who are you and why are you talking to me?"

Then Lauren recognized Hannah. "Oh, it's you,"

she said. "Don't worry, Princess. She hasn't got her nasty dingo with her."

Before Hannah could say anything, Ben held up one of the posters in front of Lauren's face. "Molly's missing. We think someone took her."

"Oh no," Lauren said. "I am so sorry. That's just awful."

The words she said were nice, but the way she said them sounded totally fake.

Lauren and Princess walked on past them. "Hope you find your dingo," she called back over her shoulder.

"Oh, we will!" Hannah said. "We will find my Australian cattle dog!"

Lauren just kept walking.

Chapter 8

Early the next morning Corey and Ben got to Hannah's house before school. They were eager to see if the plaster cast of the shoe print had worked.

Hannah opened the front door and led them straight through to the backyard.

The plastic wrap was still covering the flour mixture. Ben carefully peeled off the plastic and touched the plaster.

"Feels dry," he said. "I think it's ready."

He slowly lifted the piece of white plaster away from the ground. When he turned it over, they could clearly see the shoe print. They all grinned.

"Nice!" Corey said. "Even better than a dinosaur footprint!"

Hannah brushed dirt off the plaster cast and put

it in a large plastic bag labeled "Shoe print." "I can hardly wait to show Miss Hodges our evidence and hear what she thinks," she said.

"Speaking of evidence, I thought of something else we should have collected yesterday," Ben said. He walked over to the broken safety light and looked at the part of the light where the bulb screwed in.

"Just as I thought," Ben said, smiling.

"What is it?" Corey said. "A confession?"

"The base of the broken bulb is still in the light," he said. He put on his gloves and carefully unscrewed the metal base of the bulb from the socket. Then he put the broken piece into a jar he'd brought in his backpack.

"Good thinking," Hannah said.

"Thanks," Ben said. "And now I think we'd better get to school."

Miss Hodges was busy that day, but Club CSI finally managed to get some time with her to share their evidence. In the forensic lab, they brought out their evidence: the broken glass, the crumbs, the plaster cast, and the base of the broken lightbulb.

"Wow," she said. "I'm impressed. You've done a great job of gathering evidence."

Hannah smiled. She was still terribly worried about Molly, but she liked Miss Hodges, so it always felt good to be praised by her.

Miss Hodges picked up the jar holding the pieces of broken glass. "Let's begin with the broken glass," she said. "You might remember from class some of the ways experts can analyze glass fragments."

"They can look at the color," Corey said quickly.

"That's right," Miss Hodges said. "And so can we."

She laid a piece of black paper on a table. Then she opened the jar and carefully spread the pieces of glass across the paper.

"It looks as though all the pieces are the same color," Ben said.

"Yeah, they're all white," Corey agreed.

"Yes," Miss Hodges said. "And what does that suggest?"

"That they all came from the same lightbulb," Hannah answered.

"Right," Miss Hodges said. "Let's take a closer look."

Using magnifying glasses, they examined the

pieces of glass. Some of the fragments had printing on them.

"Like the words you see printed on the top of a lightbulb," Ben said. "The number of volts and the wattage."

"The what-age?" Corey asked.

"Exactly," Ben said.

"What do you mean 'exactly'?" Corey said. "I'm asking you what 'wattage' is."

"Oh," Ben said, getting it. "Watts are a measure of how powerful an electric lightbulb is. The more watts, the brighter the bulb."

"Oh yeah, I knew that," Corey said. "I just don't think I've ever heard anyone say 'wattage.' Wattage. The more you say it, the weirder it sounds."

They compared the glass fragments to the small pieces of glass still stuck to the base of the broken bulb. They matched.

"It seems clear that these fragments are from the broken light you found," Miss Hodges said.

Hannah thought of something. "Is there any way to tell from a broken lightbulb whether it was on or off when it broke?"

Miss Hodges nodded. "Yes, physical examination

can reveal, in some cases, whether or not a lightbulb was on when it was broken. Why do you ask?"

"Well," Hannah began. "My parents think I accidentally broke the light when I was taking the garbage out, while it was turned off. I think someone broke it after I came inside and turned on the lights. Proving that the light was on when it broke would support my theory that someone else came into my yard," Hannah explained.

"Ben, pass me that base of the lightbulb. If the filament is still intact, we can examine it and possibly determine whether or not the light was on when it broke," Miss Hodges explained as she looked carefully at the filament. After a few moments, she looked up, smiling. "Hannah, this is what investigators sometimes refer to as a 'break' in the case. Based on the condition of this filament, I can tell you with certainty that this light was on when it was broken."

Miss Hodges went on to explain that because the filament appeared distorted and damaged, it meant that the light had been on. "This is some pretty advanced lab science known as 'the tungsten trick,' but in a nutshell, the condition of the filament helps determine if the light was activated or not when the glass enclosure, or the bulb itself, was shattered. If it looked shiny and smooth, it would indicate that the light had been off," she told them.

Ben, Corey, and Hannah took turns looking at the filament closely. Ben made a mental note to research the tungsten trick to learn more about it.

For the first time since Molly disappeared, Hannah felt a little bit hopeful. "I can't wait to go home and tell my parents!" she said excitedly.

"Hey, slow down," Ben said, laughing. "We have some more evidence to get through."

Miss Hodges smiled and picked up the bag of crumbs. "So, what do we think we have here?"

Hannah said, "Well, we're not *certain*, but our theory is that they're from a crushed dog biscuit and that it's the same kind they gave out at a dog contest last weekend. Molly doesn't like them."

Ben threw up his hands in frustration. "Oh, I just thought of something! We should have brought one of those dog treats for comparison."

Smiling, Hannah reached into her backpack and pulled out a plastic bag. She held it up for them to see. Inside was a bone-shaped dog biscuit.

"Brilliant," Corey said. "You know what we should compare first? The color."

Miss Hodges gave Corey a slightly suspicious look. She was starting to notice that color was always Corey's first suggestion when it came to analysis.

When they compared the crumbs to the whole biscuit, all four of them agreed that the colors matched. There were a couple of big broken pieces whose shapes seemed to match up well with the whole biscuit.

Still, a lot of dog biscuits were the same color. And a lot of them were shaped like small bones.

"Hey, I've got an idea," Corey said. "Let's weigh the dog biscuit. Then we'll weigh all the broken pieces together and see if the two weights are close."

Miss Hodges nodded. "Corey, that's an excellent idea. We'll use the digital scales."

The forensic lab had a small set of scales that could weigh objects very accurately, down to a fraction of an ounce. Using tweezers, they picked up all the crumbs from the plastic bag and put them on the scale.

Then they weighed the whole biscuit, and it only weighed a tiny amount more than the crumbs.

"That makes sense," Ben said. "We probably left the smallest fragments in the yard. We couldn't get every single piece."

"We used tweezers," Corey pointed out.

"I mean, without using some kind of special collection tool, like a vacuum cleaner or something," Ben explained.

"The point is, the colors match," Hannah said. "The shapes seem to match. And the weight pretty much matches."

"And the smell," Corey added. "The crumbs smell like peanut butter, and so does the whole biscuit." The others sniffed the dog treats and found that Corey was right.

"Could Molly have brought the treat into the backyard herself?" Miss Hodges asked.

Hannah shook her head firmly. "I offered her one right after they gave us the bag of treats at the dog show, but she didn't like it. She just sniffed it and turned away. So I stuck our bag of treats in the cabinet."

Miss Hodges picked up the plastic bag with the white shoe print cast in it. "And so we come to our last piece of evidence."

She opened the bag and took out the plaster cast. Turning it over in her hands, she said, "This is an excellent cast. We haven't even covered making these in class yet. How did you know how to do this?"

"Dinosaur Camp," Corey said. The teacher looked puzzled.

"And I read ahead a little bit in our textbook," Ben admitted.

Miss Hodges set the plaster cast on the table. "Well, you did a great job. Now let's talk about shoe-print evidence. When we get to this part of our textbook in class, you three will be a little bit ahead of the game."

She walked over to the dry-erase board and picked up a marker. "There are three basic types of shoe prints," she said as she wrote them on the board. "Patent, latent, and plastic."

"A person leaves behind a patent print," she continued, "when they walk through something like paint or blood and leave visible prints behind."

"So this shoe print was not a patent print," Hannah said.

"Right," Miss Hodges confirmed. "A latent print

is similar to a patent print, but it isn't visible to the naked eye."

"So this shoe print wasn't a latent print, either," Ben said.

"You know, I've never understood why people say 'the naked eye,'" Corey said. "Aren't eyes always naked? You never see them wearing little shirts or hats."

Miss Hodges laughed. "That's a good point, Corey. Maybe from now on, instead of 'the naked eye,' I'll say 'the unaided eye.'"

"So our shoe print must be a plastic print," Ben said, looking at the three kinds of shoe prints their faculty advisor had listed on the board.

"That's exactly right, Ben," Miss Hodges said. "A plastic print is a three-dimensional print left in something soft, like mud or snow."

She showed the members of Club CSI how to examine a plaster cast of a shoe print for wear patterns. Since everyone walks in their own way, everyone wears down the soles of their shoes in a slightly different way.

"What kind of shoe do you think made this print?" Hannah asked.

"Yeah, and what size was it?" Corey added.

Miss Hodges shrugged. "I don't know. To find out, you'd have to ask a shoe expert."

"Do you know one?" Ben asked.

She shook her head. "I'm afraid I don't."

Corey remembered something. "My mom has a friend who runs her own shoe repair shop. Maybe we should ask her!"

Chapter 9

After school Corey led the way to the shoe repair shop his mother's friend owned. As they opened the front door, an electronic bell rang.

A smiling woman with black hair came out from the back of the small shop. "May I help you?" she asked. Then she spotted Corey. "Hi! How are you, Corey? How's your mom?"

"She's great, Mrs. Corelli. How are you?"

"I'm just fine, thank you."

"These are my friends, Hannah and Ben," Corey said, gesturing toward the other members of Club CSI "We're in a club that investigates . . . things." He thought it might make Mrs. Corelli nervous if he said they were investigating a crime.

"Nice to meet you," Mrs. Corelli said, shaking their hands.

"We were hoping you could help us, since you're a shoe expert," Ben said.

She laughed. "Well, I don't know if I'm an expert on shoes. I guess I'm an expert at *fixing* them."

Hannah pulled the bag holding the plaster cast out of her backpack. "We thought maybe you could help us with this." She took the cast out of the bag and offered it to Mrs. Corelli.

Looking curious, she took the cast and examined it. "Is this a plaster cast of a shoe print?"

"Exactly," Corey said. "We were wondering what size of shoe made this print."

"Let's see," Mrs. Corelli said, reaching for a measuring tape. "The extra plaster around the print means I can't use the Brannock Device."

"What's a Brannock?" Ben asked.

Mrs. Corelli held up a metal measuring device. Ben had seen them at shoe stores. In fact, he'd put his foot in one more than once. "One of these," she said. "The kind shoe salesmen use to figure out what size shoe you wear."

"I've seen those lots of times," Ben said. "I just never knew they were called a Brannock."

"Named after Charles Brannock, who invented them back in the nineteen twenties. He actually made the prototype with an Erector set."

"What's an Erector set?" Corey asked.

Mrs. Corelli laughed. "A kind of construction toy you're way too young to have heard of."

She used the tape measure to see how wide and long the shoe print was. She wrote down the measurements and then consulted a small chart pinned to the wall. "Ten D," she said. "That's a very common size in men's shoes."

This was disappointing news. If the shoe print had been in an unusual size, it might have helped point the way to a suspect.

"At least that proves the shoe print wasn't made by my father," Hannah said. "I checked, and he wears an eight and a half B."

"What kind of shoe made that print?" Corey asked.

Mrs. Corelli examined the plaster cast closely. "Well, it wasn't a gym shoe. Or a dress shoe. Probably more of an everyday work shoe. Maybe the kind someone would wear who's on his feet all day."

"Does the wear pattern tell you anything?" Ben

asked, remembering the term Miss Hodges had used.

Mrs. Corelli raised her eyebrows, impressed. "The wear pattern? The shoe does look worn. It's not brand-new. But it's not completely worn away, either. It might be a year or two old, I'd guess. On this foot, the right foot, the owner puts his weight on the inside of his foot. And he puts his weight forward, toward the ball of his foot, not back toward the heel."

"Can you tell how big the guy is?" Corey said.

She smiled, shaking her head. "I'm afraid not. That kind of analysis is beyond my expertise."

"You can't tell what brand the shoe was, can you?" Hannah asked hopefully.

"No, I can't tell that either," Mrs. Corelli said. "There are thousands of brands of shoes. I'm familiar with quite a few of them, and if this were a really unusual brand, I might recognize it. Especially if it had the name on the bottom!"

They laughed. She slid the plaster cast back into the bag and handed it to Hannah. The investigators thanked her and started to leave.

"May I ask what you're investigating?" Mrs. Corelli asked as they opened the door.

"A missing dog," Corey said, as if that explained everything.

Mrs. Corelli looked puzzled, but then she smiled and wished them good luck with their investigation.

Chapter 10

As they walked away from Mrs. Corelli's shoe repair shop, Ben asked, "Has anyone called about the five-hundred-dollar reward for Molly?"

"No," Hannah said. "At least, they hadn't when I left for school this morning. We can ask my parents when we get there."

Corey looked surprised. "You mean, we're all going over to your house right now?"

Hannah nodded as she walked quickly down the sidewalk. "We're going to tell them what we've learned about the evidence. Maybe then they'll believe that Molly was stolen."

Corey and Ben looked at each other. They weren't sure they wanted to be in on a confrontation with Hannah's parents. But once

Hannah got an idea in her head, there was pretty much no stopping her. Instead of wasting your time arguing, it was best just to brace yourself and go along for the ride.

They'd spent quite a while at the shoe repair shop, so by the time they reached Hannah's house, her parents were in the kitchen, working on getting dinner ready.

"There you are!" Hannah's mom said. "I was starting to get a little worried."

"Sorry," Hannah said. "I should have called. We went to a shoe repair shop owned by a friend of Corey's mom."

Hannah's mom stopped peeling carrots for a moment. "Did your shoes need to be repaired? I thought you just got those."

"We didn't actually go there to get our shoes fixed," Ben said. "We needed her expert opinion on our plaster cast of the shoe print we found in the backyard."

"Ah," Hannah's dad said as he chopped parsley. "Your investigation. How's that going?"

Hannah, Ben, and Corey told Hannah's parents what they had learned about the evidence they'd gathered. How the crumbs matched one of the dog biscuits from the dog show—the kind Molly didn't like. How the pieces of broken glass matched the base of the bulb in the safety light and how the tungsten trick proved the light was on when it was broken. And, finally, how the shoe print was made by a man who wore size 10D shoes.

After they heard everything Club CSI had to say, Hannah's parents were quiet for a moment. "Well," Mr. Miller said. "You've certainly done your homework on this one."

"I just really want to get Molly back," Hannah said. "I miss her so much."

Mr. Miller turned to his wife. "What do you think, honey?"

"I think that maybe Hannah was right about someone breaking into the yard and taking Molly," Mrs. Miller answered slowly. "It certainly would explain the things you found in the backyard. And no one's called, even though we offered the five-hundred-dollar reward."

Hannah's father nodded. "I agree with Hannah that someone may have stolen Molly. And in that

case, I think we should tell the police."

Hannah was thrilled. Her parents finally agreed with her idea of how Molly had disappeared.

"We just happen to know a very helpful policeman," Ben said.

Officer Inverno showed Hannah, Corey, and Ben into a small room at the police station. His brother was the principal at their middle school. Twice before, the three kids had done an excellent job of investigating crimes at their school. When they wanted to talk to him about a possible crime, he took them seriously.

"All right," he said. "What is it this time? Grand larceny? Arson? Murder?" He smiled to let them know he was kidding.

"Dognapping," Corey said.

"Okay," Officer Inverno said slowly. "Whose dog?"

"Mine," Hannah said. "Her name's Molly." She brought up a picture of Molly on her phone and showed it to him.

"She's a great-looking dog," the policeman said. "But what makes you think she was taken?

Could she have run away?"

"That's not what the evidence says," Corey said.

"What kind of evidence are we talking about?" Officer Inverno asked.

Hannah opened her backpack. She took out the bag with the crumbs, the jar of broken glass, the base of the broken lightbulb, and the plaster cast of the shoe print.

Together the three friends described how they'd analyzed the evidence with Miss Hodges and Mrs. Corelli. Officer Inverno listened carefully.

"And so, we believe that someone came into my backyard and took Molly," Hannah concluded.

"What do you think?" Corey asked.

Officer Inverno seemed to be choosing his words carefully. "I think you three have done a wonderful job. You've collected evidence, stored it carefully, and examined it thoroughly, even getting help from experts."

Corey frowned. "That's really nice, but why do I get the feeling you're about to say 'but?'"

The policeman chuckled. "You're right. I was about to say 'But there isn't much I can do.' All this evidence is circumstantial, not conclusive."

"Remind me of what 'circumstantial' means, please," Corey said.

"With circumstantial evidence, the circumstances *suggest* something. But they don't really prove it," Officer Inverno explained.

"So you don't believe Molly was taken?" Hannah asked, disappointed.

"She may have been," he said gently. "But nothing else was taken. And a dog is certainly capable of running away so I can't be sure a crime was committed here."

He pushed his chair back and stood up. "Still, it's good that you came in to tell me about this. It was the right thing to do. I will certainly keep all this in mind, and if any additional information comes in to really support your theory, I will definitely launch an investigation, okay?"

"Okay," Ben said. "Thanks for your time. We appreciate you listening to us."

Outside, as they walked away from the police station, Hannah felt as though she might start to cry. She missed her dog. Who knew how Molly was being treated? And it seemed the police weren't going to do anything at all to find her.

Corey and Ben could tell she was upset. "Don't worry," Corey said. "We'll find Molly."

"You keep saying that," Molly said miserably, "but it keeps not happening."

Chapter 11

As they walked back to Hannah's house, the three members of Club CSI discussed what they should do next.

"Maybe I should dress up as a dog to lure the dognapper into taking me," Corey said, hoping to get a smile out of Hannah. He didn't.

"Well," Ben said, "*we're* sure that somebody took Molly. The question is who? Let's try to come up with a list of suspects."

The three of them walked in silence for a moment, thinking. Then Hannah spoke up.

"I hate to accuse anyone without any hard evidence pointing to them," she said, "but that high-school girl Lauren seems like a suspect."

"The girl who owns that little dog? Princess?" Ben asked. "Why would she take Molly?"

"I don't know," Hannah replied. "Maybe she was jealous that her dog came in second in the contest. Since she works at a pet supply store, she might know something about how to handle dogs. And she definitely had a bag of those treats, like the smashed one we found in the yard."

"Yes, but does she wear men's shoes? Size ten D?" Ben said slowly.

"She could have worn someone else's shoes that night, just to confuse us," Corey said. "Like her dad's shoes. Maybe she even left the shoe print behind on purpose."

"I guess that's possible," Hannah said. "But now that you say it out loud, it sounds pretty unlikely."

They walked on, thinking. A kid rode by on his bicycle and waved, but they barely noticed.

"Why would anyone steal a dog, anyway?" Corey asked. "Can't you get one for free at the dog pound?"

"Some people might steal dogs in order to sell them," Ben said. "Certain breeds are really expensive."

"Including Australian cattle dogs," Hannah said. "I think my parents paid a lot of money for Molly when she was a puppy."

They reached Hannah's house. "I've got an idea," Ben said. "Maybe we should check online to see if anyone is trying to sell an Australian cattle dog. Someone around here, that is."

"That's a good idea," Hannah said. "Come on in, and we'll check."

"I've got to get home pretty soon," Corey said. "It's almost time for dinner."

"This'll only take a second," Hannah assured him. "Come on."

Hannah opened the front door and led the way into the house. Her parents heard them come in.

"What did the police say?" Hannah's dad asked.

"Officer Inverno was nice about the whole thing," Hannah said. "But he called our evidence 'circumstantial,' and he said there really wasn't much he could do."

Her dad shook his head. "I was afraid of that."

"Did anyone call about the reward while we were gone?" Hannah asked.

"I'm afraid not, honey," her mom said.

Hannah started up the stairs to her room, followed by Ben and Corey.

"Dinner's just about ready," Mrs. Miller said.

"We're just going to check something on the Internet," Hannah called. "It'll only take a second."

In Hannah's room, the three friends gathered around her computer, staring at the screen. Ben was the fastest typist, so they let him "drive."

He quickly found a few Australian cattle dogs for sale, but when they checked the pictures, none of them was Molly. And only one of them was anywhere near their part of Nevada.

Since Australian cattle dogs were a fairly unusual breed, there weren't that many of them for sale.

"Well, it was worth a shot," Ben said.

"Yeah," Hannah said. "It's always easy enough to do a quick Internet search. It's just so disappointing when you don't find what you're looking for."

"Maybe we should do a quick search for 'cute kitten,'" Corey suggested. "Then we'll get, like, a billion hits."

Hannah's mom called from downstairs. "Hannah, dinner's ready!"

"What are you having?" Corey asked. "It smells good."

Hannah smiled. "I'd invite you to stay, but you said you have to go."

"Yeah, my parents are expecting me," Corey said. "I just hope whatever they serve tastes as good as your dinner smells."

After Ben and Corey had said good-bye and left, Hannah and her parents sat down together to eat dinner. No matter what they talked about, Hannah couldn't stop thinking about her dog. Where was she? Was she all right? Was she cold? Hungry? Sad?

As she picked at her food, Hannah thought about how Molly used to sit under the table during meals. She'd bump Hannah's leg with her nose, hoping to get a bite of dinner. And whenever her parents weren't looking, Hannah would sneak food under the table to Molly. Not too much. She didn't want Molly to get fat. Just little nibbles.

She looked around the dining room, hoping to distract herself from thoughts about her missing dog, but the first thing she saw was a picture of her family with Molly. She was sitting on the ground, and Hannah had her arms around her neck, hugging her.

Hannah really didn't feel like eating.

Ding-dong.

The front doorbell rang.

"I'm not expecting anyone," Mrs. Miller said, puzzled.

"Me either," Hannah said.

Mr. Miller stood up and wiped his mouth with his napkin. "I'm not expecting anyone either, but I'll see who it is."

He left the dining room. They heard him open the front door. Then he called excitedly, "Hannah, come here!"

Hannah got up and hurried to the front hallway. When she looked through the doorway she saw . . . Molly!

Hannah ran to hug her dog. Molly jumped up and licked her face. Her dog was back!

Kneeling to pet Molly (and hug her a few more times), Hannah looked up to see who had brought her back. She was surprised to see their neighbor Mr. Webster, standing on their front step.

"Mr. Webster! Thank you so much for bringing Molly back! Where did you find her?"

Mr. Webster ran his fingers through his thinning brown hair. "Oh, um . . . down by Jackson's Pond."

Hannah was surprised. "Really? What was she doing? Was anyone with her?"

Mr. Webster looked at his shoes. "No, she was by herself. Just . . . running around. I recognized her from seeing you walk her around the neighborhood. She's a very unique-looking dog!"

Something in Mr. Webster's manner made Hannah suspicious. He wasn't looking her in the eye. And he hesitated before he answered her questions. Giving someone back a dog should have been a happy moment, but he seemed uncomfortable, as though he wanted to leave.

"I don't know if you've seen our posters around the neighborhood, but we were offering a five-hundred-dollar reward for Molly's return. You've earned it. I'll write you a check," Mr. Miller said.

Mr. Webster shook his head. "Oh no. I don't want any money from you. Just seeing your daughter reunited with her dog is enough reward for me. My daughter has a cat, and she'd be heartbroken if it was lost. I'm just happy to help."

He turned to leave. Hannah stood up to ask him another question before he left.

"Mr. Webster, I'm just curious," she said. "There's such a big park area around Jackson's Pond. Where exactly was Molly when you found her?"

Mr. Webster scratched his neck. "She was, um, near the pond."

That wasn't very specific.

"My friends and I have been doing an

investigation of Molly's disappearance, so I'd love to ask you a few more questions if you don't mind," Hannah said.

He pursed his lips. "I'm sorry, Hannah, but I'm afraid I've got to go. I'll see you later."

He hurried away down the sidewalk.

"That was odd," Hannah said. "I got the feeling Mr. Webster wasn't telling us the whole truth about where he found Molly."

"Well, wherever she was, it must have been muddy," Dad said, laughing. Hannah looked at the carpet and saw Molly's muddy paw prints.

"Oh, sorry," Hannah apologized.

"Who cares? It's only a little mud," Mrs. Miller said, joining them. "We're just thrilled to have Molly back!"

"Me too!" Hannah said, giving Molly another hug.

Molly barked with joy.

"Maybe I should put a lock on the back gate," Hannah's dad said. "I don't want anyone taking Molly away again."

"That's what's so strange," Hannah said. "Why would someone take Molly and then leave her down by Jackson's Pond?"

"Maybe they didn't like paying her food bills," Mr. Miller kidded.

"Speaking of food . . . Come on, Molly," Hannah's mom said. "Let's get you some dinner."

Hannah stopped hugging Molly and let her follow her mom into the kitchen.

"Did Molly seem all right when you were hugging her?" her dad asked. "She didn't seem hurt in any way, did she?"

"No, she seemed perfectly fine. No injuries. Her coat seemed smooth. And she seems as though she's been fed and watered," Hannah said. "Whoever took her must have taken good care of her."

"But didn't Mr. Webster say he found her alone?" Mr. Miller asked. "Maybe we were wrong. Maybe Molly did run away."

"But then how do you explain the broken light? The dog biscuit? The shoe print?" Hannah asked. "The evidence still makes me believe someone broke into the yard and stole Molly."

"I'm just glad she's back," Hannah's dad said, smiling.

Hannah went into the kitchen, where Molly was happily crunching away at her dry dog food.

"Mom?" Hannah asked. "What do you know about Mr. Webster?"

"Well, I know he's the wonderful man who returned our Molly," she said. She was sitting in a chair at the table, just watching Molly eat. It had never seemed all that interesting before, but now it was fascinating.

"What else do you know about him?" Hannah tried again.

Mrs. Miller gave Hannah a puzzled look. "You're not suspicious of him, are you?" she asked. "Hannah, he returned our dog to us. Please don't tell me you're now suspicious of him! I don't want to worry that your Club CSI is turning you into a suspicious person!"

"I'm just curious," Hannah said. "That's all."

"Well, all right. Let me think," her mom relented. "Mr. Webster lives about two blocks away. He has his own restaurant that he runs downtown. We've never eaten there, but it's supposed to be pretty good. I think maybe his wife works in the restaurant too."

"Do they have kids?" Hannah asked.

"Yes, a daughter. I think her name is Megan. She plays soccer—very competitively. I believe she goes to special soccer camps and everything."

"Oh, right," Hannah remembered. "He mentioned his daughter. He said she'd really miss her cat if it went missing, and that's why he refused to take the reward."

"He seems like a very nice man," Mrs. Miller said, as if to emphasize her earlier point.

"Yeah. *Seems*," Hannah said, thinking.

Hannah's mom sighed. "You were never this suspicious when you were concentrating on ballet."

Molly finished eating her dinner. She trotted over to Hannah and leaned against her leg. Hannah scratched her back at the base of her tail. Molly quickly moved her back leg, drumming the floor with her paw. *Thump, thump, thump, thump, thump.*

Upstairs in her bedroom, Hannah called Ben. Molly was on Hannah's bed. She wasn't really supposed to get up on the furniture, but this seemed like a special occasion.

"Molly's back?" he said after Hannah told him. "That's fantastic!"

"I know," she said. "I'm so happy."

"Maybe we should conference Corey in on this call," Ben said. "I mean, her disappearance did become a Club CSI case."

Hannah idly tossed one of Molly's chew toys onto the bed. Molly pounced on it, chewing away happily.

"You know how to make a conference call?" Hannah said.

"Sure, it's easy," he said. "But since you called me, you'll have to be the one to call Corey and then conference us all together. Unless you want to hang up and I'll call you back."

"No, that's fine," Hannah said. "I'll do it. I'd like to know how, anyway."

After Ben explained how to make a conference call, Hannah called Corey and told him the good news.

"She's back?" he yelled into the phone. "All right!"

"I'm going to bring Ben back into this conference call now," Hannah said.

"You know how to make a conference call?" Corey asked, impressed.

"Sure," Hannah said, acting like it was no big deal. "It's easy."

She pressed a button on her phone, and the

three friends could talk to one another.

"I just wanted to ask about the circumstances of Molly's return," Ben said.

Hannah told Ben and Corey about Mr. Webster bringing a very muddy Molly back and saying he found her by Jackson's Pond.

"He acted kind of weird," Hannah said. "Like he wasn't telling the truth about finding Molly."

"Do you think he could have taken Molly and returned her for the reward money?" Ben asked.

"Oh, man, I'd forgotten about the five hundred bucks," Corey said.

"He didn't take it," Hannah replied.

"WHAT?!" Corey's voice blasted into the phone. "Is he crazy?"

"He said he knew how upset his daughter would be if her pet were missing, so it was enough for him just to get me my dog back," Hannah explained.

"Well, that's really nice," Corey said.

"But you were saying you thought he was acting suspicious?" Ben asked.

"Yes," Hannah confirmed. "Especially when I asked about where he'd found Molly. I just got the feeling he wasn't telling me the truth."

Ben and Corey thought about this for a moment. Then Ben spoke up.

"Did you get a good look at his feet?"

"His feet?" Hannah asked, surprised.

"To see if his shoes looked like a size ten D," Ben said.

"Oh," Hannah said, getting it. "No, I didn't think about that. I was too excited to see Molly. That would have been a good idea."

"That's okay," Corey said. "Only Ben would expect you to check out someone's feet at the moment you were reunited with your dog."

"I just thought maybe you might have noticed. That's all," Ben protested. "But I have another idea. Did you say Molly came in with muddy paws?"

"Yeah," Hannah said. "She tracked mud all over the carpet, but Mom and Dad were so happy she was home, they didn't even get mad."

"Maybe you should collect a sample," Ben suggested.

"Of the mud?" Hannah asked, puzzled.

"Yes," Ben said. "It might give us some useful information."

"Okay," Hannah said. "I'll get some. Maybe we'd

better hang up. My parents might clean up the mud before I have a chance to collect any."

"Don't forget, you can probably collect a sample from her paws," Ben added.

"Hey, I've got an idea too," Corey said. "Maybe you should collect a stool sample from Molly, so we can figure out what she ate while she was gone."

"A stool sample?" Hannah exclaimed. "Gross!"

"I don't know, Corey," Ben said, agreeing with Hannah.

"Yeah, now that I think about it, doing the analysis wouldn't be much fun," he replied. "I hereby withdraw my suggestion."

Chapter 13

Early the next morning, Hannah took Molly for walk. The Australian cattle dog seemed very happy to be walking with Hannah again. About half of the walk was a run.

After she dropped off Molly back at the house and grabbed her backpack, Hannah headed out the front door.

"You're leaving for school awfully early this morning," her dad commented.

"I'm going to do a little investigating before school," Hannah said.

"Investigating?" he asked. "But I thought the case was closed. Molly's back. All's well that ends well."

"There are still a couple of things we're curious

about," she explained. "See you later."

Hannah closed the door and headed for Jackson's Pond.

The pond was surrounded by a large public park. There was a path around the pond, and several people were out having their morning runs.

Hannah found a patch of dirt near the pond. She took a small jar out of her backpack, knelt down, and scooped dirt into the jar. Then she screwed the lid back on, put the jar into her pack, and hurried off to school.

Miss Hodges held up the two containers to the light. "So you'd like to know if these two soil samples came from the same place?"

"Right," Hannah said. "We're trying to figure out whether Molly really was down by Jackson's Pond, the way Mr. Webster said she was."

She, Corey, and Ben had come to their faculty advisor for help with the soil Hannah had collected from the carpet and from Jackson's Pond.

"Well, I'll bet Corey can tell us what to compare first," Miss Hodges said with a smile.

"I can?" Corey said. He thought a minute. Then he grinned. "Oh! I know—color!"

"That's right," their teacher said. "First, we compare the color, starting with the naked—I mean, the unaided—eye."

She set a white piece of paper on the table. She drew a circle and labeled it "Known." Then she drew another circle and labeled it "Unknown."

"In this case, 'Known' means we know where the soil came from—Jackson's Pond," she explained. She picked up the container of soil from Jackson's Pond and poured a small amount inside the circle.

"But we know where the other soil came from too," Corey said. "Molly's paws."

"I think it's 'Unknown' soil, because we don't know where it originally came from," Ben said, "where Molly picked it up."

"That's right," Miss Hodges confirmed as she poured a small amount of the soil from the carpet into the Unknown circle.

All four of them peered at the two soil samples on the white piece of paper. They almost bumped heads.

"I don't know," Hannah said. "They're pretty close, but it doesn't seem like an exact match. The soil from Jackson's Pond seems a little lighter colored."

The others agreed. "It almost looks as though the Jackson's Pond soil has more sand in it," Ben observed.

"But I don't know if we could say they're definitely from different places based just on the color," Corey said.

"I agree," Miss Hodges said. "We need to do another test."

She went over to a small refrigerator and took out a rack of test tubes. The tubes had clear liquid in them. She carried the rack over to the table and set it down.

"I've prepared these tubes for tomorrow's class," she said. "But I made some extras, so we can use a couple of them."

"What are they?" Hannah asked.

"They're called density gradient tubes," she answered. "I've put liquid chemicals that have different densities in these tubes."

"I'm feeling a little dense right now myself," Corey said. "Remind me of what density is."

"Density is mass per volume," Ben said.

"Um, Ben? Remember what I said about using words so people can understand you?" Corey reminded him.

"If two things are the same size, but one weighs more, it has a greater density," Ben explained.

Miss Hodges pointed to the tubes in the rack. "The chemicals in the tubes have mixed in such a way that the liquid is the most dense at the bottoms of the tubes and the least dense at the tops of the tubes."

She poured a small amount of the Jackson's Pond soil in one of the tubes. It separated into three bands at different levels in the test tube. "The soil has divided into three bands of material with different densities. The denser material is lower in the tube, and the lighter material is higher in the tube."

"Right now I'm feeling like I'd be at the very bottom of the tube," Corey said.

"I think I get it," Hannah said. "We'll pour a little bit of the soil from Molly's paws into another tube. If it came from the same place, the three bands of material should float at the same levels as in the first tube. Because they have the same density."

Miss Hodges nodded and smiled. "Very good, Hannah," she said. "Would you like to do the honors?" She handed her the container of soil from Molly's paws.

Hannah carefully poured less than a teaspoon of the soil into the tube next to the one with the soil from Jackson's Pond. The soil slowly sank into the tube, settling at four different levels.

The levels did not match the levels for the Jackson's Pond sample.

"Looks like we've got a definite nonmatch!" Corey said.

The four of them agreed that the soil from Molly's paws didn't come from Jackson's Pond.

"But that means Molly wasn't at Jackson's Pond," Corey said. "She got muddy somewhere else."

"Why would Mr. Webster lie about that?" Ben wondered.

"I don't know," Hannah said. "It doesn't make sense. I mean, he brought Molly home, and he didn't even accept the reward. But he acted cagey when I asked him about where exactly he found her."

"What do you think, Miss Hodges?" Corey asked.

The teacher thought for a moment. Then she said, "It sounds to me as though Mr. Webster is a very complicated potential suspect. You need more information."

The three students nodded. "You're right," Ben said.

"Sounds to me as though we need to pay a visit to his restaurant," Corey said.

"Let's go right after school," Hannah said.

"Great idea," Corey said. "I'm always hungry after school."

Chapter 14

As soon as school let out, the members of Club CSI headed for Mr. Webster's restaurant downtown. Corey knew where the restaurant was because his family had eaten there lots of times.

"And one time, when our sixth-grade basketball team won the district championship, we got to go there for our celebration dinner," he added.

"What's it called?" Hannah asked.

"I think we just called it 'the celebration dinner,'" Corey replied.

"No, I mean the restaurant," Hannah explained.

"Webster's," Corey said.

"Yes, Webster's," Hannah said, thinking Corey was asking her whose restaurant she meant.

"Right," Corey said.

Hannah waited a minute for an answer. When she didn't get one, she asked again, slightly frustrated, "So, what's it called?"

"I told you!" Corey said. "Webster's!"

Ben cut in to help make things clearer. "What Corey means is that Mr. Webster's restaurant is called Webster's."

"Oh," Hannah said, finally understanding.

"I think it's named after his family," Corey said.

"I didn't think it was named after the dictionary," Hannah retorted.

"That's a good theory too," Corey said.

It was a pretty long walk. They had plenty of time to plan what they were going to do.

"We're going to have to approach Mr. Webster tactfully," Ben said, shifting his backpack on his shoulders. He wished he'd packed fewer books into it before setting out on this hike downtown.

"What do you mean?" Corey said.

"We can't just barge into his restaurant and accuse him of lying," Ben explained. "If we do that, he might refuse to tell us anything at all."

"But you agree he's lying about where he found

Molly, right?" Hannah said, pausing to take a pebble out of her shoe.

Ben and Corey waited for Hannah. Corey took an apple out of his backpack and started eating it.

"That's what the density gradient tube seemed to indicate," Ben said.

"Also, you said he acted suspicious," Corey added between bites.

"Right," Hannah said. She got her shoe back on, and they resumed walking.

"I've been wondering if the reason he didn't take the five-hundred-dollar reward was that he felt guilty," Ben said.

"Please don't mention that five hundred dollars," Corey protested. "It just makes me sad."

They passed a trash can, and Corey tossed the apple core with a little hook shot.

"Still," Ben said, "we have to remember that Mr. Webster is innocent until proven guilty."

"I know that," Hannah said. "It's not like I'm going to walk in there and put him in handcuffs."

"I've gotta admit I hope he's not guilty," Corey confessed.

"Why?" Hannah asked.

"Because the food at his restaurant is really good," Corey explained. "I'd hate for that place to shut down."

"Don't worry," Hannah assured Ben. "I'll be tactful."

They walked on for a few more blocks. "We're almost downtown," Hannah noticed. "Which way is Webster's restaurant?"

Corey pointed down the street. "We go up to that stoplight and turn right. The restaurant's in the middle of the next block."

"That's good," Hannah said. "My backpack's killing me."

Ben's backpack was killing him too, but he didn't admit it.

They made their way to the stoplight and turned right. Soon they spotted a sign that read WEBSTER'S. Club CSI headed down the block to the restaurant.

Inside, there were only a few customers seated at tables and booths. Late afternoon seemed to be a slow time for the restaurant.

Hannah walked up to a woman who was the hostess . . . and the only waitress. "Excuse me—" she started to say.

"Would you like a table?" the woman asked, smiling.

Hannah smiled too. She figured Ben's warning about being tactful applied to everyone who worked at the restaurant.

"No, thank you," she said politely. "We were just wondering if we might be able to talk to Mr. Webster for a minute."

The woman looked surprised. "Sure. He's in the kitchen. Just a second."

She checked in with her customers, to see if they needed anything, and then went through a swinging door and into the kitchen.

"I wonder if we'll get any free samples," Corey thought aloud.

"I doubt it," Ben said.

The door had a round window in it, and Hannah saw Mr. Webster look through to see who had asked to see him. When he saw it was Hannah and her friends, he didn't look happy.

But when he walked through the door, he was smiling. He gave Hannah a little wave.

"Hello!" he said cheerfully. "How's that beautiful dog of yours?"

"She's good," Hannah said. "Thanks again for bringing her back, Mr. Webster."

"No problem."

Hannah realized Corey and Ben were just standing there. "Oh, these are my friends, Ben and Corey."

Mr. Webster shook their hands. "Nice to meet you, Ben, Corey. Wait a minute. Haven't I seen you before, Corey?"

"My family comes in here all the time," he said.

Mr. Webster nodded. "Right. I remember now. Your dad always gets the rib-eye steak. Welcome back."

"Do you think it might be possible for us to talk to you in your office, Mr. Webster?" Ben asked.

"Uh, sure," Mr. Webster said, looking slightly puzzled. "But I can't talk for very long. We've got to get ready for the dinner rush."

"It will only take a couple of minutes," Ben assured him.

"Okay," Mr. Webster said. "Follow me."

He led the way through the kitchen to a tiny office. The four of them could just barely squeeze into the room.

"So, what did you want to ask me? Are you looking for jobs in a restaurant?" he asked.

Hannah smiled, remembering to be tactful. "No,

we were just curious about something. You said you found Molly down by Jackson's Pond, right?"

Mr. Webster looked very uncomfortable. "Right," he said.

"We did this little experiment where we compared some dirt from the park at Jackson's Pond to the dirt Molly had on her paws when you brought her back," Corey chimed in.

"Oh, yes?" Mr. Webster said. He was holding his mouth in a tight line.

"The weird thing was," Corey said in his friendliest manner, "the two dirt samples didn't match. Odd."

Mr. Webster ran his fingers through his hair. "I don't understand why you're telling me about dirt samples."

"Well," Ben said carefully. "It's just that because the samples didn't match, we were thinking that maybe you didn't really find Molly down by Jackson's Pond. Maybe that was a . . . mistake. Perhaps you found her somewhere else."

Mr. Webster was quiet for a minute. Then he said, "Okay, you got me."

Ben asked, "So you didn't find Molly by Jackson's Pond?"

"No," he said.

Hannah felt a flash of anger. If there had been a window in the office, tact would have flown right out of it.

"You lied to us!" she cried. "Did you steal my dog?"

Mr. Webster looked shocked at Hannah's accusation. "No!" he said vehemently. "I would never steal anything! I found your dog, remembered who she belonged to, and returned her to you, safe and sound."

"Then why did you lie about where you found her?" Hannah pressed.

Mr. Webster sighed and looked embarrassed. "Fine," he said. "I didn't tell you where I found your dog, because I really shouldn't have been there."

"Where did you find Molly?" Ben asked.

"Pine Field," he said.

"Pine Field?" Corey repeated, puzzled. "I used to play soccer there when I was a kid. Why shouldn't you have been there?"

Mr. Webster puffed out his cheeks and then blew air through his lips. Finally, he said, "Because I was spying."

"Spying?" Hannah asked. "On whom?"

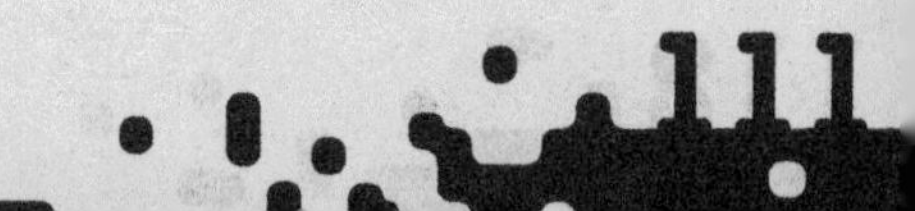

"Look," he said. "I love my daughter. And my daughter loves soccer. So I went down to Pine Field to spy on the team my daughter's team is going to be playing this weekend. I thought maybe I could gather some information that would be useful to her. And then I spotted your dog. Well, naturally I wanted to return Molly to her owner, but I was embarrassed about being at Pine Field to spy on a rival soccer team. It sounds silly. I'm embarrassed saying it now. So I just changed the location of where I found her. There aren't any soccer practices at Jackson's Pond. I didn't think a little white lie would hurt anybody."

The Club CSI members felt a little embarrassed themselves. They'd insisted on getting the truth from this man, but the truth didn't have anything to do with Molly's kidnapping.

"Thanks for telling us the truth, Mr. Webster," Ben said.

"Yeah, we're sorry we embarrassed you," Hannah chimed in. "I just really want to know what happened to Molly."

"And you don't have to feel ashamed about spying on a rival team," Corey said. "I've played on lots of

teams, and the coaches are always checking out the other teams, trying to figure out their plays."

Mr. Webster stood up and led the three friends back through the kitchen to the front door of the restaurant. "Actually," he said, "I feel better. I'm glad you kids got me to tell the truth."

"In that case," Corey said, "I'm sure you won't mind answering one more question. What size shoe do you wear?"

Mr. Webster looked confused. "Eleven and a half. Why do you ask?"

"No reason," Corey said. "See you next time!"

As they walked out of Webster's restaurant, Ben asked Corey, "Didn't you believe Mr. Webster's story?"

"Oh, yeah, absolutely," Corey said. "He seemed totally believable."

"Then why did you ask him his shoe size?" Hannah asked.

Corey grinned. "Because it never hurts to be superthorough."

Chapter 15

"As long as we're being superthorough, maybe we should go over to Pine Field," Ben suggested.

"What for?" Corey asked. "To spy on a soccer team?"

"I bet I know why," Hannah said as they waited for the stoplight to turn green. "To pick up a soil sample."

"Right," Ben said. "If the soil at Pine Field matches the soil from Molly's muddy paws, that'll support Mr. Webster's story."

The light changed. The three friends crossed the street.

"Okay," Corey said. "But I'm sure he was telling the truth this time. It embarrassed him to admit

he'd been spying on a soccer team. Also, I'd just like to mention that it's a long walk from here to Pine Field."

Hannah laughed. "So that's the real reason you don't want to be superthorough this time—the long walk."

"But I thought your basketball coach wanted you to get lots of conditioning," Ben pointed out.

"Yeah, well, Coach wants me to cut back on sugar, too, but that's not happening either," Corey said. "Besides, walking isn't conditioning. Running is conditioning."

"Do you want to run?" Hannah asked.

"All the way to Pine Field?" Corey asked. "No way!"

They walked another block. Then Hannah had an idea.

"Let's stop off at my house and get Molly," she said. "Maybe she'll pick up a scent or lead us to something."

"Your house is kind of out of the way," Corey protested.

"We could drop off our backpacks," Hannah suggested. "And maybe grab a snack . . ."

"Your house it is," Corey agreed.

Pine Field was more than just a field with pine trees around it. Maybe that's what it had started out as, but now it was a big park with a soccer field, a baseball diamond, and tennis courts.

Molly tugged on her leash when she saw the park. She wanted to run—to jump over obstacles, dash through tunnels, and weave around poles.

Hannah knew what Molly wanted. And secretly, Hannah wanted that too. She would've loved to do some agility training with her dog in the park. But that's not why they were there.

"Sorry, Molly," Hannah apologized. "No training today. But if you'd like to show us how you ended up here, that'd be great."

"Instead of just *understanding* two hundred words, it'd be real helpful if Molly could *say* two hundred words," Corey said.

"Let's get that soil sample," Ben replied.

"Where should we get it?" Hannah asked. "It's a pretty big park."

"Well, Mr. Webster said he was watching a soccer team. . . ." Ben recalled.

"*Spying* on a soccer team," Corey corrected.

"So, why don't we collect the soil sample near the soccer field?" Ben suggested.

"Good idea," Hannah agreed. "Come on, Molly. Let's run."

As soon as she heard the word "run," Molly took off, dragging Hannah behind her. Hannah had to sprint to keep up, and she couldn't sprint forever. Luckily, the soccer field was nearby.

Corey and Ben trotted to the soccer field. "Guess I'm getting that conditioning after all," Corey said.

Ben knelt down and scooped a few spoonfuls of dirt into a small jar. Since they'd formed Club CSI, he'd started carrying plastic bags, gloves, spoons, and small glass jars in his backpack at all times. He never knew when he might encounter important evidence. (Which was why he hadn't dropped off his backpack at Hannah's house, though he'd unloaded a couple of his heaviest textbooks.)

Ben dug through his backpack and pulled out two jars of dirt. He read their labels and stuck one back into the pack. The jar he kept was full of the mud Hannah had collected from Molly's paws.

Ben held up the two jars to the sunlight,

comparing their color. Hannah and Corey looked too. Molly sniffed the ground.

"The color seems to match," Ben said. "When we get back to the forensic lab, we could do another density gradient tube analysis. But just based on appearance, it looks as though the dirt from Molly's paws matches the dirt here at Pine Field."

"So Mr. Webster was telling the truth," Hannah said.

"Told you so," Corey said smugly.

"You were the one who asked him his shoe size!" Ben exclaimed.

"Superthorough," Corey replied with a smile.

They decided to let Molly lead them around, to see if she had anything to show them. But she just wandered the soccer field, happily sniffing the ground.

Eventually, Molly took them away from the soccer field, toward the bathrooms and water fountains. There was also a kiosk where you could put up signs and posters.

"Isn't that Ryan?" Corey asked.

Ryan was a red-haired guy in their grade at Woodlands Junior High School. He was putting up a hand-lettered poster. As they got closer, they could

see what the poster said: MISSING DOG.

That seemed like a pretty big coincidence.

Club CSI hurried over to the kiosk. "Hi, Ryan!" Corey said, waving.

Ryan turned around. He recognized his three schoolmates. "Hi," he said. Then he pointed to the poster. "You haven't seen my dog, Pepper, have you?"

They shook their heads. "I'm sorry your dog's missing," Hannah said.

"Thanks," Ryan said. "I really miss him."

"I know how you feel," she replied. "Molly here just disappeared too."

Molly sat at Ryan's feet. He patted her head. "How'd you get her back? The pound?"

"No, a neighbor of ours found her at Pine Field and brought her to our house," Hannah explained. "But we think someone else dognapped her."

"Dognapped her?" Ryan repeated. "That's terrible." Then he looked more closely at Molly. "Hey, wait a minute. I recognize this dog. You won O'Brien's contest last weekend!"

"How do you know that?" Hannah asked.

"I was in the contest too. I mean, Pepper was. We didn't win, but he did great."

So, Ryan's missing dog was in the contest too. That was *way* too big of a coincidence.

"Pepper played a little bit with your dog," Ryan said, remembering. "But there was another dog he really liked—a little terrier. I think I heard her owner call her Princess."

Hannah looked at the picture of Pepper on Ryan's poster. He was kind of a plain-looking brown dog. She didn't remember him, but during the contest, she was too busy concentrating on Molly to notice all the contestants.

"Pepper's brown all over?" Hannah asked.

"Except for his chest," Ryan said. "He's got a white patch in the shape of a pepper shaker. That's why we named him Pepper."

Corey looked puzzled. "Isn't a pepper shaker the same shape as a salt shaker?"

"Yeah," Ryan agreed. "But it'd be weird to call your dog Salt."

"True," Corey said. He tried it out, calling, "Here, Salt! Come, Salt! That's a good boy, Salt!"

Ben wanted to get back to the specifics of the case at hand. "What were the circumstances of Pepper's disappearance?" he asked.

Corey thought Ben sounded a little too formal, like he was a police detective or a lawyer in a courtroom. But Ryan didn't seem to mind at all. He wanted to talk about his dog's disappearance.

"Yesterday afternoon, I let Pepper out into the backyard to do his business," Ryan said.

"Your dog has his own business?" Corey asked. "Oh, wait. I get it."

"He likes to be outside, so I went upstairs to my room to play video games."

"Which game?" Corey asked.

"Last Combat."

"Awesome game," Corey said, nodding.

"How long was Pepper out in the backyard?" Hannah asked, steering the conversation back on track.

"Only about half an hour," Ryan said. "There's a bell by our back door that Pepper can jump up and ring when he wants to come back in. He's really smart."

Hannah smiled and nodded.

"When I didn't hear the bell ring after half an hour, I decided to go down and check on him," he continued. "I went out into the backyard, and he was gone. I went all around the neighborhood calling his name, but I never found him. I don't know how he ran so far in such a short time. He *is* fast, though."

"Maybe he didn't run," Hannah murmured.

"What do you mean?" Ryan asked, frowning.

"Would you mind if we took a look at your backyard?" Ben wondered.

"Not at all," Ryan said.

"Right now?" Corey asked.

"Sure," Ryan said. "Let's go."

Chapter 16

It turned out that Ryan lived close to Hannah, so they dropped off Molly at home on their way to Ryan's house.

Ryan's family lived in a small, white, two-story house. As the four middle schoolers made their way up the front walkway, Hannah noticed one of the A Dog Lives Here stickers from the contest in the window.

They hurried through the house and out the back door into the yard. There was a high wooden fence around the backyard.

"Could Pepper have jumped over the fence?" Ben asked.

"Or dug under it?" Corey added.

Ryan shook his head. "No way," he said. "Pepper's a good jumper, but he can't jump that high. And I looked all around the fence to see if he'd tunneled under it, but he hadn't. See for yourself."

Corey, Ben, and Hannah walked along the fence looking for holes in the ground or gaps between the boards. There weren't any. The fence was in good shape.

"When I came out to look for Pepper, the back gate was open," Ryan said.

The four of them went to examine the gate carefully.

"And you're sure the gate was closed when you let Pepper out into the backyard?" Ben asked.

"Positive," Ryan said firmly. "I'm real careful about that."

Hannah couldn't help but be reminded of when her family had asked her if perhaps she had accidentally left their back gate open. "Was the gate locked?" she asked gently.

"No," Ryan said. "We don't have a lock on the gate. Maybe we should. I'm thinking of asking my parents to get one, so we can lock Pepper in from now on. After he comes back. *If* he comes back." As he said the last sentence, Ryan's face clouded over.

Hannah touched Ryan's arm. "Don't worry," she said. "He'll be back."

Ben had opened the gate and was looking at the other side of it, the side facing the alley. He examined the whole gate. The last part he checked was the edge with the latch on it. He started at the top and then worked his way toward the bottom.

He spotted something.

There was a tiny piece of red fabric stuck to the gate. Ben pulled on his rubber gloves, pried the red scrap off the wood, and put it into a plastic evidence bag.

He proudly held up the bag to show the others. "Look at this," he said.

Hannah, Corey, and Ryan gathered around.

"What is it?" Ryan asked.

"Looks like a little piece of red cloth," Corey said. "Pepper wasn't wearing anything when he disappeared, was he?"

"Just his collar," Ryan answered. "And it was black leather, not red cloth."

Ben peered through the plastic bag at the evidence. "One edge of the cloth is jagged. It looks as though maybe the gate ripped this fabric from a piece of red clothing as someone rushed through the gate."

Hannah suddenly remembered something and snapped her fingers. "Lauren," she said. "She's always wearing her red high-school sweatshirt."

"Yes," Ben said slowly. "But lots of people wear red."

"True, but she was already a suspect," Hannah said. "Remember how nasty she was about Molly?"

"Suspect?" Ryan said. "Suspect of what?"

"Dognapping," Corey said.

"You mean you think this Lauren is stealing dogs?" Ryan said, getting angry. "My dog? Who is she? I want to talk to her."

Ben felt as though Club CSI was losing control of their own investigation. "Hold on," he said. "We don't know for sure Lauren's done anything wrong at all. We need to investigate more."

"I just want my dog back," Ryan said. "The sooner the better."

"We know," Hannah said reassuringly. "And the minute we find out anything about where your dog is, we'll let you know."

Ryan thanked them and gave them his phone number. As they walked away from his house, the three friends discussed what to do next.

"I'm just not sure we have enough evidence that

we can confront Lauren," Ben said.

"Where do they sell those sweatshirts for the high school?" Corey asked.

"I think they have them at Werner's," Hannah said. Werner's was the oldest clothing store in town. "Why?"

"I was just thinking we could compare the color of the fabric piece to the color of one of those sweatshirts," Corey said.

"Again with the color," Ben said, smiling.

"I think that's a really good idea," Hannah said. "You'd be surprised how many shades of red there are in clothing."

"Really?" Ben said. "I thought red was red."

"No," Hannah said. "If we can perfectly match the scrap of fabric to one of those sweatshirts, that'll be an important piece of forensic evidence."

They turned a corner, heading toward Werner's.

At Werner's a smartly dressed young woman asked, "May I help you?"

"Do you have Woodlands High School's hooded sweatshirts?" Hannah asked.

"We certainly do," the saleswoman said cheerfully.

"In that far corner. Follow me."

As they made their way past displays of shirts, pants, and dresses, Ben asked, "Does the clothing manufacturer ever change the shade of red the sweatshirts come in?"

"Oh no," the saleswoman said. "They're very consistent, because the color of the sweatshirts has to match the school's colors exactly."

They arrived at a display of Woodlands High School apparel for girls. Several styles of sweatshirts hung on racks—all the same shade of red.

"Here we are," the saleswoman announced brightly. "May I help you find a particular size?"

"No, thank you," Hannah said politely. "We'll browse around a bit and look for you if we need you."

"That's fine," she said, smiling. "I should be right over there." She pointed to a counter with a cash register.

The woman walked away. As soon as she was gone, Ben pulled the plastic bag with the red fabric sample out of his backpack.

He held it up against a hooded sweatshirt, like the one they'd seen Lauren wearing both times they'd run into her with Princess.

"I'd say that's a definite match," Corey said. "But I'm no expert on shades of red. I defer to Hannah's superior sense of color."

Hannah looked at the scrap and the sweatshirt closely. "Exactly the same color," she announced. "And the fabric looks the same to me, too."

"Sounds to me like it's time to have a talk with Lauren," Corey said.

As they walked out of Werner's, leaving the disappointed saleswoman behind, Ben said, "I'm not sure it's such a good idea to confront Lauren."

"Why not?" Corey asked. "I know she's in high school, but she's only, like, five foot one. She doesn't scare me."

"I know," Ben said. "But stealing dogs is a pretty serious crime. Maybe we should include the police."

They walked on for a minute or two, thinking about what to do.

"You know, speaking of Lauren only being five foot one, I seriously doubt she wears a man's size ten D shoe," Corey pointed out.

"Maybe she had an accomplice," Hannah

suggested. "Maybe she got some big guy from her high school to help her."

"All the more reason to bring Officer Inverno in on this," Ben said.

"Come to think of it, we forgot to tell the police we got Molly back," Hannah realized.

"I think that settles it," Ben said. "To the police station?"

"To the police station," Corey agreed. "But if we walk anywhere after that, you may have to carry me on your shoulders."

Chapter 17

The policeman at the front counter of the station hung up his phone. "I'm afraid Officer Inverno isn't available right now. Would you like to talk with another officer?"

The three members of Club CSI looked at one another. They were all thinking the same thing: They didn't want to talk to another officer. They wanted to talk to Officer Inverno. They'd reported Molly's disappearance to him, so they wanted to continue the case with him.

Ben turned back to the policeman behind the counter. "Do you know when Officer Inverno might be available?"

The policeman shrugged. "I'm not sure. He's interviewing a witness."

"We'll wait, thanks," Ben said.

The three friends sat down on a bench to wait. Corey was hoping they'd see criminals being escorted in and out of the station, but it seemed really quiet.

"I've been thinking about Lauren's motivation," Ben said.

"What about it?" Hannah asked.

Ben shifted on the wooden bench. It wasn't comfortable. "Well, you thought maybe Lauren took Molly because she was jealous Molly won the dog contest, beating her dog, Princess."

"Right," Hannah said, nodding.

"But why would she take Pepper?" Ben asked. "He didn't win the contest. He didn't even beat Lauren's dog. Didn't you say Princess came in second?"

"That's true," Hannah said. "I don't know."

"Maybe once she got a taste for stealing dogs, she really liked it," Corey suggested.

A man came through a door from inside the station. He was followed by Officer Inverno.

"Thanks again for your statement," Officer Inverno said. "We really appreciate it."

"No problem," the man said.

"The prosecutor will be in touch," Officer Inverno

continued. "She'll let you know if she needs you to appear in court."

Officer Inverno noticed Ben, Hannah, and Corey. They'd jumped up from the bench the minute they saw him.

"Well, hello!" he said, smiling. "Are you waiting to see me?"

"Yes. Do you have a minute to talk with us?" Hannah asked.

"I sure do," the policeman said. "Come on back."

He led them through the doorway, down a hall, and into the same room where they'd met before. They all sat down.

"What can I do for you?" Officer Inverno asked.

"Remember my dog, Molly?" Hannah asked. "The one who was missing?"

"Of course," he said.

"Well, she's back," Hannah said.

"That's great! Glad to hear it!" he said, smiling. "So the case is closed."

"Not quite," Ben said. "Now a different dog has gone missing."

They told him about Ryan's missing dog, Pepper. Officer Inverno looked skeptical.

"Well, I doubt the two missing dogs have anything to do with each other," he said. "Dogs go missing every day."

Ben took a plastic bag out of his backpack. It held the small scrap of red fabric. He handed it to Officer Inverno, who held up the bag and peered at it. "Looks like a scrap of material."

They explained how they had found the scrap on the gate at Ryan's house and how it matched the Woodlands High School sweatshirts.

"Okay," Officer Inverno said, drawing out both syllables. "What does that tell you?"

They told him about Lauren, and about how she always wore a red Woodlands High School sweatshirt.

He wasn't convinced. "This evidence is pretty"—He was going to say "flimsy," but he didn't want to hurt their feelings or discourage them from exploring forensics—"light. And didn't you show me a plaster cast of a man's shoe print?"

Hannah was impressed he remembered that detail from Molly's disappearance. "Yes, but I was thinking maybe Lauren had an accomplice."

"So, what is it you'd like me to do, exactly?" Officer Inverno asked.

"Come with us to talk to Lauren," Corey said.

"Right now?" he asked, surprised. "Do you even know where she is?"

Hannah was already looking up the number of O'Brien's pet supply store on her phone. She called the number.

"Hello?" she said. "Is this Lauren? Oh, hi. We were just thinking about coming down to O'Brien's. My friend has some more questions about—"

She put her hand over the phone and hissed, "What do you call those lizards you're interested in?"

"Axolotls," Ben said. "But they're not lizards—"

"Axolotls," Hannah said into her phone. She listened for a moment. "Great! We'll see you there!" She ended the call and said, "Lauren's working at the store right now. Could you go there with us? Please?"

Officer Inverno thought about it. He wasn't convinced by any means that this high-school girl was stealing dogs. All the three kids had to go on was a tiny scrap of red fabric. On the other hand, cases had been solved on tiny pieces of evidence before. And these kids had a good track record. They'd been right before.

"I'm glad you came to me," he said. "I don't like the idea of you going around accusing people of crimes." He sighed. "Okay, let's go."

"Great!" Corey said. "Um, would you mind driving? I'm sick of walking."

Chapter 18

Club CSI enjoyed riding in Officer Inverno's police car. He even agreed to stop off at Hannah's house on the way and pick up Molly.

"It's okay," he said as Molly jumped into the backseat. "I'm a dog lover myself."

"Why do you want Molly to go?" Corey asked.

"I'm not sure," Hannah said. "Just a hunch."

They parked a block away from O'Brien's. "I don't want to spook anybody," Officer Inverno said. "Think you can handle the walk, Corey?"

"Just barely," Corey said. "But don't tell Coach."

The shop was small but tidy, with everything neatly arranged on clean shelves. A sign said customers were welcome to bring their pets in with them.

"That means you, Molly," Hannah said. Molly wagged her tail and trotted right into the store.

Lauren looked up from a magazine. She was startled to see Hannah, Ben, Corey, and a policeman. "What's going on?" she said. "Get that dingo out of here!"

"Your sign says pets are welcome," Corey pointed out.

"Pets, not wild beasts," Lauren said.

Ben watched Molly carefully to see if she looked mad or scared when she saw Lauren (or smelled her, knowing dogs). But Molly ignored Lauren completely. She seemed much more interested in all the bags of dog food, sniffing around them and checking the floor for any dropped pieces.

Officer Inverno gave Lauren a friendly smile. "Hi, Lauren," he said. "I'm Officer Inverno. I just wanted to ask you a couple of quick questions."

Hannah couldn't help but step forward. She already suspected Lauren of stealing her dog, and Lauren's comment about Molly being a wild beast made her even madder.

"Why did you steal Molly and Pepper?" she asked accusingly.

"I didn't steal anything," Lauren snapped. "And who are Molly and Pepper?"

Officer Inverno tried to intervene. "Now, Hannah, I really wish you'd let me handle this."

But Hannah took another step closer to Lauren. "You know perfectly well who Molly and Pepper are. Molly's my dog and Pepper belongs to Ryan. They were both in O'Brien's dog contest. And you stole them!"

Lauren looked totally confused. "You're crazy," she said. "I have a wonderful little Norwich terrier. Why would I want to steal your stupid mutts?"

Hannah yanked the bag with the square of red fabric out of Ben's backpack and held it right in front of Lauren's face. "Then how do you explain *this*?" she barked.

"A plastic bag?" Lauren said, mimicking Hannah's tone.

Hannah opened the bag and took out the scrap of red fabric. "We found this piece of red material on the gate to Ryan's yard," she said, holding it against Lauren's sweatshirt. "And it perfectly matches your sweatshirt!"

"So what?" Lauren said. "Get away from me!"

Lauren turned away from Hannah. Corey pointed at the back of her sweatshirt, near the bottom hem.

"Look!" he said. "There's a hole!"

Lauren whipped back around. "What are you talking about?"

Officer Inverno stepped forward. "Lauren, would you mind if we look at the back of your sweatshirt for a second?"

Lauren folded her arms. "Yes, I do mind. This is harassment."

"Are you afraid we'll find something that proves you're guilty?" Hannah asked.

"Of course not! Because I'm not guilty of anything!" Lauren said. She sighed, then turned around to let them examine the back of her sweatshirt.

Corey quickly found the hole he'd spotted. Hannah held up the scrap of red fabric to the square hole. The piece fit perfectly.

"See?" Hannah said. "It matches. That proves Lauren tore her sweatshirt on the gate to Ryan's backyard." Satisfied, Hannah placed the piece of fabric back in the plastic bag.

"No, it doesn't!" Lauren insisted. "I've never even been in this Ryan's backyard. In fact, I don't even know which Ryan you're talking about!"

"Do you know how you tore your sweatshirt,

Lauren?" Officer Inverno asked.

"*I* didn't tear it," she said. "Someone else must have. I left my sweatshirt here, in the store, overnight, and when I looked at it the next morning, there was this tear in it."

Ben didn't think this sounded very likely. "So, you didn't tear your sweatshirt. Someone else did. But you don't know who."

"That's what I said, dork," Lauren said, sneering.

"Okay, okay," Officer Inverno interjected, holding up his hands. "There's no need for name-calling. Lauren, I'd appreciate it if you'd come with us back to the station."

Lauren looked stunned. "Seriously? Are you arresting me? Because of a torn sweatshirt?"

"No," he said. "But this is a serious matter, and I'd just like to ask you a few more questions."

"Can't you just ask me here?" Lauren said. "I'm trying to work."

"I'm afraid the store where you work really isn't the best place for questions," Officer Inverno explained.

"But I'm the only one here right now," Lauren protested. "I can't just leave. I'll get fired."

Officer Inverno was about to speak when Molly suddenly ran into the rear of the pet supply store, barking. She had been sniffing the floor, making her way toward the back. Now she had run through an open door leading to a back room.

"Molly!" Hannah called. "Where are you going? Molly, come!"

Usually Molly was very good about immediately obeying commands. But she stayed in the back, out of sight, barking and barking.

"It's like she's found something," Ben remarked.

"That's just where Mr. O'Brien boards the dogs," Lauren said.

They all rushed into the back room. The room was full of big cages with dogs in them. Molly was barking at the dogs, who had started barking back at her. It was loud.

In one of the cages, Hannah recognized . . .

Pepper! Ryan's missing dog!

Chapter 19

"That's Pepper!" Hannah cried. "Ryan's dog! I recognize him from the poster!"

Hannah kneeled down, slid back the latch to the cage, and opened the door. Pepper came running out, wagging his tail and licking Hannah's face. She wasn't his owner, but she knew his name, and he was thrilled to see anyone who let him out of that cage.

"Are you sure it's Pepper?" Officer Inverno asked. "Looks like a plain brown dog to me." He looked at the tag on the cage Pepper had just come out of. "And the tag here says 'Buddy.'"

Hannah pointed to a white patch on Pepper's chest. "See this mark? Where his fur is white?"

Officer Inverno nodded.

"See how it's shaped like a pepper shaker? That's what his family named him for."

"Watch this," Corey said. "Hey, Buddy!" The brown dog paid no attention at all. "Hey, Pepper!" The dog immediately turned and trotted over to Corey.

"I'm sold," Officer Inverno said. "He's Pepper."

Molly and Pepper sniffed each other and tried to play together, even though there wasn't much room to play in the back area.

Corey noticed brown crumbs in the bottom of the empty cage Pepper had been in. He picked one up and sniffed it. It smelled like peanut butter.

He noticed a couple of the other dog cages had brown treat crumbs in them too.

"Lauren, what do you know about Pepper being kept in a cage here?" Ben asked.

"Nothing," she said. She looked totally bewildered. "I thought his name was Buddy. These are the dogs Mr. O'Brien boards for people who are going out of town for work or for vacation. Maybe the tag on the cage got switched or something. Maybe someone put this dog in the wrong cage. I have no idea."

"Are there records for all the dogs who are boarding here?" Officer Inverno asked.

"Sure," she said. "On the computer."

"Let's take a look, okay?" Officer Inverno said with a friendly voice.

Lauren went back out front to the computer. She used the mouse to click through a couple of screens.

"Is there a record for Pepper?" Officer Inverno asked.

Lauren typed "Pepper" into a search box and hit return.

"Nope," she said. "Nothing here for Pepper."

Pepper looked up every time someone said his name.

"How about for Buddy?" Ben asked.

"Good thinking," Corey said, giving a thumbs-up.

Lauren typed "Buddy" into the search box. No results.

"There's no record for a dog named Buddy, either," she said. "That's really weird."

"It's not all that weird, considering that Ryan's family never boarded Pepper." Hannah countered. "The question is, how did Pepper get here?"

"Don't look at me," Lauren retorted. "I have no idea how he got here. I don't have much to do with the boarded dogs. I just work at the store in front."

Hannah looked at Lauren sharply, trying to gauge whether she was telling the truth or lying.

"I wonder if there are any other dogs back there who aren't in the computer," Corey said.

Ben headed back toward the room with the cages. "That's a good question," he said. "Let's find out." Corey followed him through the door.

In the back room Ben pulled a pen and small notebook out of his backpack. "Read me the names on the cages," he instructed.

"You got it," Corey said. He went from cage to cage, reading out loud all the names of the dogs, so Ben could write them down. It wasn't always easy for Ben to hear the names with all the dogs barking, but Corey repeated each name until they'd listed them all.

Ben took the list of dog names back to Lauren. "Could you—"

"Check to see if they're in the computer? Absolutely," she said, getting right to work. Lauren actually seemed as eager to find out what was going on with the dogs in the back as Club CSI was.

As Lauren rapidly typed names into the computer, Hannah felt her suspicion of the high-school girl

melt away. If Lauren was acting, she was a really good actress. She should get all the leads in her school's plays and musicals.

"There are two other dogs in the cages with no records in the computer," Lauren said. "Rocky and Brody."

They all went back to look at Rocky and Brody. Rocky was a boxer, and Brody was some kind of spaniel. In the bottoms of their cages, there were brown crumbs from peanut-butter dog treats.

"I think Brody's a springer spaniel," Hannah said. Before her family got Molly, they researched lots of dog breeds together.

"If Brody's even his name," Ben said. "The tag on Pepper's cage said 'Buddy,' so maybe these names are wrong, too."

"Did you check these dogs in when their owners brought them to be boarded, Lauren?" Officer Inverno asked.

"No," Lauren said. "Mr. O'Brien must have checked them in. But I don't get why he wouldn't put them in the computer."

Officer Inverno nodded slowly. "I'd like to talk to Mr. O'Brien. Do you know where he is?"

Lauren shook her head. "He said he'd be right back. I thought he'd be here by now."

They heard a door open. It was the front door to the store.

Lauren went back out front. The others followed her—even Molly and Pepper.

A tall, balding man had entered the shop. "Any customers while I was gone?" he asked.

Then he saw Officer Inverno. He froze.

"Mr. O'Brien?" the policeman asked.

Instead of answering, the man turned and ran out of the store.

Chapter 20

"Hold it!" Officer Inverno shouted at the man. The police officer ran through the store, knocking a bag of dog food off a shelf as he passed, and out the front door.

Without even thinking, Corey took off running after them. He may have walked a long way that day, but his legs still had some running left in them. His coach would have been proud.

Molly started to run out too, but Hannah stopped her. She didn't want to risk losing her dog again. Soon Molly and Pepper were much more interested in the spilled dog food than the chase outside.

Mr. O'Brien wasn't in great shape. After a couple of blocks, he was huffing and puffing. He stopped running in front of a bakery. He bent over and put his hands on his knees, gasping for breath.

As customers in the bakery watched through the windows, Corey caught up with Mr. O'Brien. Officer Inverno was right behind him.

Corey thought Officer Inverno might pull out his gun from its holster, tell Mr. O'Brien he was under arrest, and handcuff him. But he didn't do any of those exciting things. Instead, he put his hand on Mr. O'Brien's arm and helped him to stand up straight.

"Well, I guess we've had our exercise for the day, Mr. O'Brien," Officer Inverno said. "Now let's head back to your store for a little talk."

Hannah, Ben, Lauren, and Molly were waiting out in front of the pet supply store. Officer Inverno led Mr. O'Brien inside, and the others followed.

"He isn't talking," Officer Inverno said. "On the way back here, he didn't say a word."

"Why should I say anything?" Mr. O'Brien asked. "I haven't done anything wrong."

"Then why'd you take off running when you saw Officer Inverno?" Ben pointed out. "Did you

suddenly get the urge to exercise?"

"Maybe I forgot to feed the meter," Mr. O'Brien replied, sneering.

"He didn't put any money in a parking meter," Corey said. "I watched him the whole time—on the run out and on the walk back."

"He doesn't have to feed the meter," Lauren said. "He's got his own parking place in back of the store."

Mr. O'Brien glared at Lauren. "Do you like your job here, Lauren? Do you want to keep it?"

Lauren glared right back. "I used to like it, but I don't think I do anymore. As a matter of fact, I quit! "

She crossed her arms and stood there defiantly.

"If you quit, why don't you leave?" Mr. O'Brien grumbled.

"Because I can't wait to see what happens," Lauren said.

Pepper walked over to where the group was standing, crunching on one last piece of spilled dog food. "Do you know this dog, Mr. O'Brien?" Corey asked.

Mr. O'Brien glanced at Pepper. "I don't think so."

"Then why was he in a cage in the back of your store?" Ben asked.

The man shrugged. "How should I know?" he said, sounding bored. "Maybe Lauren put him there."

Lauren's jaw dropped. "I did not! I can't believe he's trying to blame this on me!"

"Blame what?" Mr. O'Brien said innocently. "I really don't see anything wrong here. Except for some brown mutt wandering around my store when he should be in a cage."

While she listened to Mr. O'Brien deny everything, Hannah had been getting madder and madder. She stepped forward.

"Do you remember me, Mr. O'Brien?" she asked, looking him right in the eye. He looked away. "My dog, Molly, won your contest."

Hannah put her hand on Molly's head. Molly sat right by her side.

Mr. O'Brien looked back at Hannah. "Yeah, I remember. Your dog did the agility tricks. Very well trained."

"Did you steal her?" Hannah asked point-blank.

Mr. O'Brien snorted. "Of course not. Don't be ridiculous. Why would I steal your dog?"

"I don't know," Hannah said. "But whoever did left behind some good, strong evidence that they

broke into our backyard and took Molly."

Mr. O'Brien's eyes narrowed slightly when Hannah said "evidence."

Hannah reached into Ben's backpack and pulled out a jar with broken glass in it.

"We collected this glass from the safety light the dognapper accidently broke," she said. Mr. O'Brien looked unimpressed.

Hannah pulled a plastic bag out of Ben's backpack. "We also collected these crumbs from a broken dog biscuit in the yard."

Ben chimed in, "When we analyzed the crumbs, they perfectly matched the organic peanut-butter treats you gave away at the contest."

A muscle in Mr. O'Brien's jaw tightened. Hannah reached into Ben's backpack again and removed the plastic bag with the square of red fabric in it.

"We found this scrap of red fabric stuck to the back gate at our friend Ryan's house. His dog, Pepper, was stolen. And we found Pepper here in your store."

Mr. O'Brien's shoulders slumped a little.

Corey joined in. "The piece of fabric matches the tear in that red sweatshirt Lauren's wearing—the one she left overnight in the store."

Hannah turned to Lauren. "Do you think Mr. O'Brien could have borrowed your sweatshirt, Lauren?"

"Definitely. Dogs always love me, and I bet he figured my sweatshirt would help lure the dogs to him because it has my scent on it," she told Hannah. Then, looking at Mr. O'Brien, she said, "Dogs can also always smell a rotten person!"

Mr. O'Brien gave Lauren an angry look. "She doesn't know what she's talking about," he said. He looked back at Hannah. "It sounds as though you kids have had a grand time playing detective—picking up pieces of glass and dog biscuits and red cloth. But none of this has anything to do with me. You haven't proved anything."

He shot a quick glance at Officer Inverno. The policeman was looking slightly doubtful.

"Actually," Ben said. "The dog biscuits do have something to do with you. You gave them out at the contest. You also gave out stickers saying 'A Dog Lives Here.' The houses Molly and Pepper were stolen from both had those stickers."

Mr. O'Brien shook his head and smiled. "So what? You've got a real active imagination."

Hannah pulled one last plastic bag out of Ben's backpack. "Here's something we didn't imagine." She took the flour plaster cast of the shoe print out of the bag.

"What's that?" Mr. O'Brien asked.

"The dognapper left a shoe print in Hannah's backyard," Ben explained. "We made a plaster cast of the shoe print."

Mr. O'Brien looked worried.

Corey leaned down and peered at Mr. O'Brien's feet. "I'd say you wear about a . . . ten D?"

Mr. O'Brien did have pretty large feet that looked like they could've been a size 10D. He was wearing brown work shoes—comfortable shoes for someone who was on his feet all day.

Officer Inverno stepped forward. "What do you say, Mr. O'Brien? Should we compare this plaster cast to your shoe? See if the tread matches?"

"And the wear pattern?" Hannah added.

Mr. O'Brien looked trapped. He took a deep breath and let it out. "Look," he finally said. "Business has been terrible. I thought maybe the contest would help bring in new customers. But then, right after the contest, three of the companies I owe money to all wanted to be paid. Right away. Or I'd lose my business."

He nervously rubbed his neck as he spoke. "I thought reward money would be a quick way to raise some cash. I planned on paying it back someday."

He looked at Ben, Hannah, and Corey. "I've gotta admit, you kids are smart. You figured it all out. I went to the houses with the stickers in the windows. And I tempted the dogs out with the treats."

Mr. O'Brien looked down at Molly. "Unfortunately, Molly here didn't like the treats. I had to grab her, and as I left the yard, I broke the light. She was too athletic to hold on to, though. The first chance she got, she broke free and ran off.

"I didn't want to have that kind of trouble with Pepper. I remembered he liked Lauren's dog at the contest, so I borrowed her sweatshirt when I went to take him. I figured maybe the sweatshirt would smell like Princess, and Pepper would like that, so he'd be easier to grab. And I was right. He was no trouble at all."

"That reminds me," Hannah said. "I've got to call Ryan and tell him we found his dog." She pulled out her cell phone.

"All right, Mr. O'Brien," Officer Inverno said. "You need to come down to the station with me."

The policeman led Mr. O'Brien away. Hannah finished

talking to Ryan on the phone. She turned to Lauren.

"I'm sorry we suspected you of being involved," she said. "Thanks for helping us find the real dognapper."

"Well," Lauren said, "I'm sorry too. Sorry I called Molly a dingo." She leaned down and petted Molly, who thumped her tail on the floor. "I was wrong about you. You're not a beast. You're a sweetheart!"

At the park that weekend, Molly and Princess had a great time playing together. The other stolen dogs had been returned to their families, who were thrilled to see them again. It had been a very satisfying case to solve.

As they watched the two dogs run and tumble in the grass, Ben said, "You know, Molly was a big help. She was the one who ran into the back room and found Pepper and the other dogs. Maybe we should make her the fourth member of Club CSI."

Hannah laughed. "Maybe," she said. "But I don't think Miss Hodges will let her into the forensic lab."

"And I'll tell you one thing," Corey added, "I'm not sharing my treats with her!"

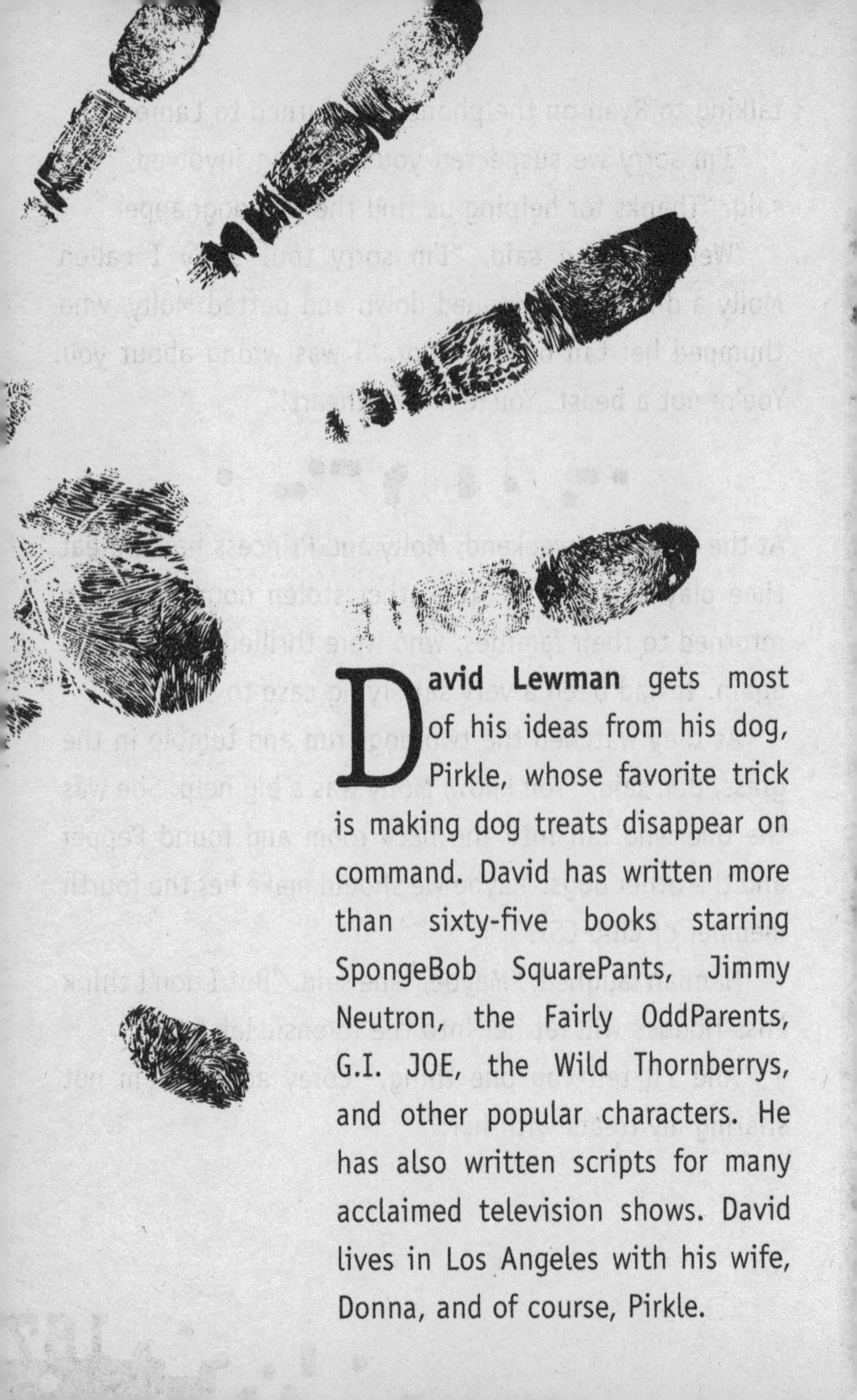

David Lewman gets most of his ideas from his dog, Pirkle, whose favorite trick is making dog treats disappear on command. David has written more than sixty-five books starring SpongeBob SquarePants, Jimmy Neutron, the Fairly OddParents, G.I. JOE, the Wild Thornberrys, and other popular characters. He has also written scripts for many acclaimed television shows. David lives in Los Angeles with his wife, Donna, and of course, Pirkle.